Olympian Passion

A romance by

Andrya Bailey

To everyone who is passionate about the magic of love at first sight.
Believe.

To my loving parents.
And to the reason of my existence - H.

Contents:

Acknowledgments

A special thanks to all my friends who have encouraged me to write romance. I deeply appreciate all of you who motivated me, supported me and offered suggestions, feedback and your valuable time.

Luzia Ferreira: for sharing with me the passion for the muse, from beginning to end.

Edward M. Wolfe: for his priceless feedback and editing suggestions, helping me shape some of the most challenging scenes.

Fern Brady: for her invaluable feedback, suggestions and support.

To all my wonderful Beta readers who took their time to read and provide me with helpful insight.

To the muse who is inspiring me to create this trilogy.

To my wonderful editor.

To all my readers: for your amazing reviews and support. All my love.

Chapter 1

At that fraction of a second, when my eyes found him, I felt Eros' arrow hitting my heart with an intensity I'd never experienced before. I thought I was seeing a mirage: tall, muscular body, tousled black hair, wearing a light blue button down shirt - which complemented the tan of his olive skin – a black jacket and dressy black pants. The man looked exactly like a hero from Immortals, or one of the perfectly chiseled statues of Apollo or Zeus I often found myself contemplating in museums.

I'm a helpless romantic, always believing in love at first sight, thinking about the day my prince in shining armor would come trotting down to capture my heart. Or, rather, when my Greek god would descend from Mount Olympus to take me as his own venerated and immortal goddess. Greek mythology has always been one of my favorite subjects, and books about the glorious myths of gods, sagas and quests in search of love, beauty and immortality abound in my library. I love reading and looking at pictures, dreaming about this far gone world of intrigue, jealousy and passion, imagining the handsome gods seducing virgin nymphs, morphing into mere mortals or other forms, to enrapture the object of their lust into their sometimes fatal embraces. Wandering through museums, I often stared musingly at the formidable marble statues of mythological gods and heroes with their lean, muscular, perfectly toned and chiseled male bodies. I wondered when I'd have my chance to go to Greece and lose myself in the Parthenon, in Athens, or the Temple of Poseidon at Sunion, or the best-preserved Greek temple in the world, the Temple of Hephaestus, to meet my fantasy, the Olympian god of my dreams. I had no idea I would find him so close to home.

A few days ago, I received a call from Dr. Jones, the museum's director, advising me I had been accepted for the internship at the Museum of Fine Arts. I was beside myself with excitement. That's the reason I took the summer off from my Art History school teacher job: I had really been looking forward to this opportunity. I was graduating the following year and getting my Master's degree in Classical Studies at Rice University in Houston, so this break might even help me get a job at the museum. The invitation to attend the Greek Bronze Vessels special preview party followed and I couldn't believe how lucky I was. It was the first time this collection was coming to the museum, and I was hoping my internship would include working with the curators in the Antiquities department. I was doing research about Greek vessels for my thesis, so that was a most welcoming coincidence.

Jane, my best friend, was waiting for me by the front entrance when I arrived at the museum for the party.

"You look great, Sabrina," she said when she saw me. "I can't believe we were invited to this wonderful party, and I can't wait to see the new exhibit. Let's have a glass of champagne and some hors d'oeuvres before Dr. Jones starts the announcements."

We accepted a flute of champagne from the bartender and walked around the large foyer, which was being used as the background for the cocktail party.

"My beautiful ladies," we heard Curt exclaim. Our adorable, friendly classmate approached us with open arms to give us a hug. His friend Robert, who was with him, gave us each a peck on the cheek.

"This is so amazing, isn't it?" Curt asked. "I'm dying to go inside the exhibit room and see the Greek vases. Are you all excited about the internship? I can't wait to start."

"It's like a dream come true. When Dr. Jones called me, I was beside myself. I'd love to work in the Antiquities department," I said. A waiter came by with a tray of fresh fruits and cheese and we each grabbed a handful to munch on.

That's when I saw the mirage, the fabulous looking god of my dreams on the other side of the room, across from where we

2

were standing. Dr. Jones offered him a glass of champagne and he accepted it with grace, bowing respectfully. I had no idea who the seductive god-like creature was, but for me, it was love, or lust, at first sight. Like magic, I felt a bolt of lightning going through me. At that moment, I knew I had been hit by a love arrow, and I almost choked on a grape.

"Sweetie, are you OK?" I heard Robert asking me, while tapping lightly on my back. I gulped the rest of the champagne to stop the coughing.

"Yes," I mumbled, my eyes fixed on the sexy man on the other side of the room. "I'm fine, thanks, Robert."

Dr. Jones walked up to where a microphone was set up, and the room fell silent, waiting for him to start. He introduced the new interns, including me, and the new fellows who were visiting during the summer, following with a brief lecture about the exhibit we were there to see. The man of my dreams remained at a close distance from Dr. Jones, and I still had no idea who he was. All I was sure of is I had never seen him in the museum or the university before.

"Dr. Nikos Soulis," I heard Dr. Jones say. The man walked up closer to Dr. Jones. "I want to extend our welcome to Dr. Nikos Soulis, a Greek archaeologist, scholar and curator of Antiquities from the National Archaeological Museum in Athens, which ranks among the top ten museums in the world, for his invaluable contribution helping us bring the Greek Bronze Vessels exhibit to our institution. He will be with us for the next two months, overseeing the exhibit."

The Olympian god looked at the audience who was clapping for him and bowed, showing a soft smile that almost made me faint. I was totally hypnotized by this man's charm and charisma. His eyes were deep and penetrating, and he had a serious and commanding persona. I couldn't believe a Greek god had fallen from Olympus and landed right in front of me.

"Thank you, Dr. Jones, and I'd like to thank all of you for such a welcoming reception. I sincerely hope you enjoy the exhibition," Dr. Nikos Soulis said, in an accent that made my heart skip a beat. I was paralyzed, as if I had stared into Medusa's eyes and been turned into stone.

The halls were opened and we were allowed into the exhibition. Curt and Robert split from us, and I walked in with Jane, trying to disguise my nervousness. All I could think of was Dr. Nikos Soulis. I spotted him by himself inspecting one of the bronze vessels and wanted to approach him; however, I was not bold enough to strike up a conversation with him. It would be so easy to start talking about the Greek vases, after all that's what I was doing my research on. But this man, even from a distance, had an intimidating effect on me. Besides, I didn't want to feel like a fool for falling in love with a stranger upon first sight. I can't believe how my legs were shaking and how strong my heart was pounding just to be watching him. Out of nowhere, Curt and Robert approached the vessel Dr. Soulis was examining and got into a conversation with him. Instead of walking through, Jane stopped by them, and pulled me into the group where I was introduced to the attractive stranger.

"Sabrina, have you met Dr. Soulis? He's our special guest with a Master's in Archeology and a Doctorate in Ancient Greek Art, and he's here with the bronze vessels. Isn't it fabulous?" Curt said, pulling me closer to Dr. Soulis. The Greek god glanced at me with eyes framed by luscious long lashes that made them darker and more mysterious, and extended me his hand. His touch was electrifying. He bowed his head like he had done before while he was introduced by Dr. Jones to the guests, and shook my hand, showing a faint smile again. Like butter, I was melting easily under his hot and smoldering gaze.

"Nice to meet you. Please, call me Nikos, don't bother with the title," he said with that accent that had made my heart skip a beat. "Are you interested in Greek art?" he asked.

"Interested?" Jane exclaimed before I could answer. "She LOVES Greek art, Dr. Soulis, I mean, Nikos. It's her main field of study. I'm sure you could give her a lot of guidance during her internship. What a beautiful coincidence!"

4

He studied me quietly. His faint smile appeared again and I didn't know what to say. It was embarrassing yet exciting to know I might have the opportunity to spend some time with the stunning god during his visit, discussing my favorite field of study. It would be absolutely divine.

"Is that so?" he asked, tilting his head and looking at me with intensity.

"Yes, I'm... I'm getting my Master's degree in Classical Studies next year and I'm doing research about these vases for my thesis," I managed to say.

His eyes met mine for a moment too long and I felt butterflies in my stomach. I turned my eyes away from his, and my stare fell upon the beautiful ancient bronze vessel in front of us.

"Beautiful piece, isn't it? This bronze vessel is one of the earliest vessels we have in the collection, dating to the ninth or eighth centuries B.C. If you're doing research about it, you're probably aware these bronze vessels were made in a wide range of shapes. This one, for example, is a tripod," he lectured.

We all faced the artifact and studied it, agreeing with what he had just said.

"It was used as a cooking pot, wasn't it?" I asked.

"Yes," he replied. "But it could also be given as a prize for winners in athletic contests," he continued, speaking about it with the confidence of someone who might have lived in those ancient times.

"Ha, there you are. I've been looking for you all over the place," Maggie exclaimed, bursting suddenly into our group, grabbing him by the arm and whisking him away, as if she was the girlfriend who was jealous of her boyfriend's popularity. She was also one of our classmates, the rich heiress of a prominent art collector and museum benefactor. "I'm sorry guys, but I have to introduce Dr. Soulis to some of the curators and professors, see you later."

He looked at us with an apologetic expression, but didn't offer any resistance and was taken away, barely having time to bow us goodbye. Maggie looked amazing. She was slim and tall, wore her long blond hair loose, and was dressed in a gorgeous silver cocktail dress with matching silver long heeled sandals. I couldn't help feeling a hint of jealousy when she took Nikos away from us like that, so intimately.

"Everyone wants to meet him. After all, he's the expert in Greek art. He knows everything about this exhibit and helped put it together, of course," Curt said after Nikos was out of sight.

"I'm sure his time here will be busy and well spent," Jane said. "But why is Maggie all over him?"

I was glad Jane was the one who questioned Maggie's interference. Although I was curious with the way Maggie intruded into our group and kidnapped Nikos away, I decided not to ask anything. I didn't want it to appear too obvious I was infatuated with someone I had met for the first time in my life minutes before.

"They're probably going out already. Maggie doesn't waste her time when she sees a hunk like him," Curt said. "She always finds a way of going out with the interesting guys."

"Do you think? He looks so handsome… and Maggie is the social one, isn't she?" Jane said.

"Well, let's take a look around. These objects are stunning, look at that vase!" Curt exclaimed, and walked towards another piece. "I'd love to work with Dr. Soulis while he's here," he said. Robert followed him but I stayed behind for a few more minutes contemplating the bronze vessel the Greek god had been appreciating when I first spotted him in the gallery. I didn't notice Jane was still standing next to me.

"It would be great if you could work with him, wouldn't it?" she asked.

"Yeah, it would, especially if I could get his help with my research," I said absentmindedly.

"I hope you do. I'm sure there are lots of students lining up to have a chance to talk to him, but you should ask Dr. Jones about it first thing tomorrow. Come on, let's look around," Jane said.

We followed the rest of the group, and had a great time appreciating the beautiful collection of Greek vases. I tried to find out where Maggie had taken Nikos, but I didn't see them again for the rest of the evening, and I was eager for the morning. Anticipating I might work with this Olympian vision for the whole summer was beyond my wildest dreams, and I couldn't wait to find out.

Chapter 2

Early the next morning, I rushed over to the museum to find out where I was going to be placed during my internship, hoping to work with the Antiquities department and have a chance to meet with Dr. Nikos Soulis. While I thought about how wonderful it would be to see him again, I came across Jane in the main entrance.

"Jane, did you have your meeting yet? Do you know in which area you will be doing your internship?" I asked her, curious about the placements.

"Hi, girl! Yes, I found out I will be working with the curators in the Asian department, and I couldn't be happier." She sounded excited. Jane was a beautiful Asian American girl. Her parents had migrated from Taiwan and she had a special interest in Asian history. "I hope they pair you up with the Greek archaeologist," she continued. "I think his knowledge and native experience will be a plus for you to learn more from. Besides, he looks like a hero from the mythology books, and I know you love that look."

I wasn't expecting her to mention Nikos so soon. "He does look like a hero from mythology books… doesn't he? I'd love to work with him. I have so many questions already, especially knowing he has done work in Greece as an archaeologist."

"In fact, it looks like it will be hard to find time to work with him if you don't get an appointment. He is booked solid with several meetings, classes, lectures and seminars throughout his visit, according to Maggie," Jane said. "Can you believe I bumped into her a few minutes ago? I'm not sure why Maggie knows so much about his agenda. She seems to be guarding him like she's protecting a relic."

That was an interesting observation. "Is she on the internship program, too? Maybe she's assigned to work with him," I said, trying to hide my disappointment.

"She's not participating in the internship program," Jane responded. "That's why I'm wondering why she knows so much about Nikos. She is volunteering as a docent in the museum during the summer, but she's not involved with the program. She's not even remotely associated with the Antiquities curatorial department. Her area of interest has nothing to do with the classical arts," she explained. "Curt thinks they're dating, you know, and it's possible, knowing Maggie…"

"Oh, well," I said. "I hope I get some time assigned to spend with him, for the sake of my research and thesis. I guess I'll find out soon. I'm meeting with Dr. Jones right now," I told her. "I'll catch up with you later."

"Before you take off, do you have any plans for this evening?" Jane asked.

"I was going to spend the evening at home studying. I need to work on my research paper. Why?"

"We're going out – guess where? To Theo's, the Greek restaurant, mind you. Well, with this entire Greek theme going around, it's the absolute thing to do, right? So come meet us, it's a small group," she said.

"Not a bad idea to go out for Greek food, but I won't stay long. What time are you guys meeting up?"

"Around 6:30 pm. See you there, then. Good luck in your meeting," she said warmly.

I walked up to the conference room thinking about what Jane had said. Was Nikos' Maggie's love interest? I couldn't find any other feasible explanation to it if what Jane said was true. If Maggie was not involved in the internship program and was working as a docent volunteer during the summer, why would she be so concerned, or rather, so involved with his schedule?

The door to the conference room was open when I arrived, and Dr. Jones, the short, bald man wearing thick glasses and dressed in an impeccable striped navy blue suit was sitting at the table waiting for me. I stepped in, trying to focus my mind on my internship to leave any thoughts of Nikos behind. After I greeted him, he invited me to sit down.

"I'm so glad to have you here as an intern this summer, Sabrina," he started, offering me a glass of water. "I heard you've been doing research on the Greek vases for your thesis next year. You want to specialize in Ancient Greek Art, correct? It's a fascinating field," Dr. Jones said.

I nodded and smiled at him. "Ancient Greek Art has always been one of my favorite areas, Dr. Jones, and I'm delighted to be able to see the Greek Bronze Vessels exhibit. I really hope I have a chance to learn more about it and work with the curators. In any case, I'm really looking forward to this internship, regardless of what area I'm assigned to," I said, trying to disguise how eager I was to work with the Antiquities department.

"We are very fortunate this year to host a colleague from Greece. You might remember I introduced Dr. Nikos Soulis last night at the opening reception," he said. "He's here for the next two months and will be able to share his expertise with us. He came specifically because of the Greek Bronze Vessels exhibit. As you probably heard, he helped put it together and is responsible for several of the pieces that came from the museum where he works. We are working on the possibility of a long term loan of some of the pieces as well."

I gulped in anticipation, and took a sip of the water he had offered me a few minutes earlier. Was this his prelude to announce my teaming up with Dr. Nikos Soulis' department? I definitely hoped so. I nodded again, waiting for him to continue.

"However, there's something I need to tell you," he paused for a moment, stood up and walked to a closet at the end of the conference room. He picked up a folder from one of the shelves and walked back to sit at the table facing me. "Dr. Soulis' schedule is extremely tight. We knew of his coming before you were granted the internship, but unfortunately I did not anticipate the need for changes in his schedule." He searched for something inside the folder he had just picked up, found a piece of paper and studied it for a few minutes. I remained silent, afraid I would say something that would show my utter disappointment. "You have actually been assigned to work with the Arts of Africa, Oceania, and the Americas' curatorial department. This department deals with the art of the peoples of sub-Saharan Africa, the Pacific Islands, and North, Central, and South America as you are aware of. It is one of our largest departments." He sounded cheerful, or maybe he was trying to sound positive so I would not be frustrated for not having been assigned to work with the department I was mostly interested in.

"That's fantastic, I'm very thankful for the opportunity to further my education in this department," I lied.

"But I'm looking at the schedule here," he said, pointing to the paper he had been studying while talking to me, and removing his thick glasses before continuing. "And I really want to see if there's something we can do to pair you up with Dr. Soulis before he leaves. I believe it will be very beneficial for you to have at least a one on one session with him and get some of his expert insight into Greek art, taking advantage of our current exhibit, of course."

"I will be extremely thankful to have this chance, Dr. Jones. I would really appreciate having some time to talk about my research with an expert who works at the National Archaeological Museum in Athens." I was elated. This would be an incredible opportunity.

"I can't tell you when exactly," he said, while he cleaned his glasses with a piece of cloth he removed from his pocket, "but I'll study his schedule and I will try to fit you in without overwhelming Dr. Soulis. He has so much to offer and we booked him solid for the whole time." He stood up and put his glasses back on, ready to finalize the meeting. "I see there's some scheduled free time to show him around the city with one of our volunteers, and I'm sure he wouldn't mind canceling it to help a brilliant student like you," he said, walking me to the door. "I'll get back to you on that. I have to talk to him and see what we can arrange. Enjoy your internship, and once again, welcome."

He shook my hand and after thanking him for his time, I left with renewed hope. Even though I was frustrated because I wasn't assigned to work with the Antiquities curatorial department, there was still a chance I would get to meet with Nikos for a one on one session.

I participated in several meetings throughout the day and was hoping to bump into my Greek dream, but it didn't happen. He never came out of his hiding place, maybe he was not even in the museum. I wondered where he was and who were the lucky people he was spending time with? And suddenly, I felt like an idiot for thinking so much about a guy I had only seen once. What was wrong with me? I had to stop feeling like that. I knew nothing about Dr. Nikos Soulis. What if he was dating Maggie? Get real, I told myself.

Even if I had a one on one session with him within the next few weeks, what would I get from it besides a good lecture on ancient Greek bronze vessels from an expert? Whatever strong attraction I fostered for him would not manifest into a sexual relationship. It would remain in the platonic realm. There was no time and place for it. He was going back to Greece in two months, and besides, there was no sign whether the attraction was mutual. He probably wouldn't even remember me if he saw me again. But I wanted to find out why I felt such an irresistible attraction to this man. Was it really love at first sight? Was he my Greek god who had descended from Olympus? If I insisted on it, I knew I was headed into an incurable heartache but it might be worth it.

Chapter 3

I got home tired and didn't feel like going out to Theo's, but Jane texted me to let me know she had made reservations and they were waiting for me, even if it was just for a little bit. The restaurant was not far from the museum area where my apartment was located, and it would not take me long to get there. I took a quick shower, dressed in a pair of jeans and a short sleeve blue blouse, tied my long brown hair in a pony tail, chose a pair of high heeled sandals to match the blouse and was on my way. Theo's was the place to be and was buzzing with people. I finally spotted Jane, Curt and Robert sitting at a large table at the back. Jane had made a reservation for six people, but two of them canceled the dinner. I wiggled my way to the table.

"I'm so glad you made it!" Jane exclaimed upon seeing me.

"I almost gave up, but hunger won," I said, taking my place at the table. They were talking about their day at the museum, and where they were placed for their internship. Curt was the lucky one who had been assigned to work with the Antiquities curatorial department.

"I already got my schedule," he said, "and I'll be participating in a research group with Dr. Nikos Soulis. I can't wait. Rumors have it that he worked on an archaeological site back in Greece and even found some objects from the eighth century B.C., the same era most of the bronze vessels in this exhibit came from." Curt was elated. He loved archeology and had always wanted to meet a field archaeologist, plus the fact that Nikos Soulis was from Greece made it even more exciting for him. And who wouldn't be excited? I felt a bout of momentary jealousy; after all, Curt was going to participate in a research group with my Olympian dream.

"This would have been right up your alley, Sabrina. Too bad you didn't make the cut earlier. But I'm sure Dr. Jones will try to fit you in with Nikos' schedule." Jane tried to sound reassuring.

"Hey, talking about the devil… the love birds are coming," Curt said, looking towards the front entrance of the restaurant where Nikos and Maggie were just walking in.

"Wow, there's Maggie… with Nikos," Jane said. "Let's call them to sit with us. We have two extra chairs anyways, unless they're looking for a romantic evening…"

Curt waved and called their attention to our table. Maggie looked around as if searching for something else, maybe another empty table to avoid coming to sit with us. After a moment, she grabbed Nikos' hand and led him over to our table. We all stood up to greet and shake hands. My heart was pounding so fast I was glad everybody was talking at the same time, so he could barely hear my faulty voice when I said it was nice to see him again. It was more than nice, I was thrilled, but I had to compose myself. My reaction was ridiculous; I couldn't just feel like a virgin teenager every time I saw this guy. I had to try to bury these feelings as much as I could. Maggie had held hands with him, they were together, which meant he was off limits to my romantic illusion.

"How do you like Houston?" Curt asked Nikos when he had sat down.

"It's very different from Athens, of course, but I like the dynamics. It's a welcoming change of culture," he responded, sporting a knock out smile that did nothing to ease my anxiety.

"Nikos has yet a lot to see and visit, and I'm making sure he doesn't miss anything," Maggie blurted out. I had a feeling Nikos rolled his eyes at her, but it had to be just an impression.

"So bringing him to a *'Greek'* restaurant is making sure he doesn't miss anything?" Jane asked sarcastically.

Maggie gave her an annoyed look. "Theo's is the place to be, you know that. I thought he would be interested in seeing how Greek food is becoming so popular here."

"We're just having fun," Nikos said, trying to dissipate any hint of animosity between the two girls. "Have you guys ordered yet?" He picked up a menu from the table and studied it.

14

"You should make a suggestion for all of us," Jane challenged him. "I wouldn't know for sure what was authentic Greek or not. Would you mind?"

He smiled that absurd smile of his again. I couldn't help but stare at his sculptured facial features and those dark, enigmatic eyes.

What kind of effect did he have on me? I was completely under this man's spell. And he didn't seem to take notice of me in any particular way.

The table was soon filled with an array of appetizers ordered by our Greek guest: plates of moussaka - an eggplant dish; spanakopita - spinach and feta pies; dolmades - grape leaves stuffed with meat; keftedes - herb enriched meatballs served fried with tangy marinara sauce; and a bowl of salad with feta cheese, tomato, cucumber, oregano and olives. I ordered tzatziki, a cucumber yogurt dip as an appetizer, and Theo's specialty homemade chicken and orzo soup. I had lost my appetite when I saw Maggie holding hands with him, but I had to eat something or it would look awkward.

"My grandmother cooked the best chicken and orzo soup," he said, looking at me. "It's one of my favorite soups. I hope you enjoy it."

I looked at him, shyly. "I'm sure I will," was all I could mutter.

Curt got Nikos engaged in an animated chat about the project they would both be working on, while I ate in silence, trying to pay attention to the conversation, still in disbelief that I hadn't been chosen to work in his department.

"And how did you meet him? You're not participating in the internship program, are you?" Jane blurted out suddenly, probing Maggie about her relationship with Nikos.

"Not this year, no. I decided I would do some volunteer work instead. I'm involved in other projects at my father's organization right now and I didn't want to be tied up for the internship the whole summer," Maggie responded, avoiding the first question concerning how she had met Nikos. I knew Jane would not let it slip.

"Did you meet Nikos in the   museum?" Jane insisted.

15

"In the museum, yes, of course," Maggie answered, glancing furtively at Nikos. She seemed to be avoiding the subject, while at the same time looking for his approval to talk about it. Nikos was engrossed in a conversation with Curt and wasn't paying attention to her. "I've been taking him around to show him the city - driving him to the museum, to meetings, you know, making sure he feels welcome."

Maggie wasn't eager to provide much information about her relationship with Nikos, even though something was going on between the two of them, so Jane backed off. I finished my appetizer and my soup, which was indeed delicious, and was ready to go.

"Your suggestions were really good. Thank you. I loved the soup," I told Nikos before I got up to leave.

Nikos was surprised to see me getting up so soon. "Are you already leaving?" he asked. "Dr. Jones mentioned you need help with Greek Antiquities, but unfortunately your internship is not in my department."

"She wanted so much to get into Antiquities, but Dr. Jones had other plans for her." I wasn't surprised Jane would interrupt and say something, as usual.

"No, I got a really interesting department to work with. But it would have been nice to be in Antiquities. I'm working on a research paper about the Greek bronze vessels, and I know you're the expert," I said. "Dr. Jones might try to work something out for me to have a session with you, if possible."

"Nikos' schedule is totally full, Sabrina, he barely has time to breathe in that museum. If I were you, I wouldn't count too much on it," Maggie said dryly.

"I'll wait for Dr. Jones' call. It was nice seeing you all, have a great night," I said, walking away from the table. I couldn't stand the way Maggie was acting. She was so possessive of Nikos.

"Wait, Sabrina, let me walk you to your car," Nikos said, and to my astonishment, he followed me out of the quaint and busy restaurant. I shuddered to think he was coming after me, and I had no idea what to say when we got to the parking lot. My

Olympian god was right there in front of me and there was no one around us.

"It is true that my schedule is full, but I will make an effort to see to your needs. It is very rewarding for me to know a student is so interested in my field of expertise. That's what motivates the teacher, you know," he said.

"I'd… like that opportunity very much, Nikos," I said, avoiding his hypnotizing eyes.

"I will personally talk to Dr. Jones, and we will arrange something. In the meantime, here's my local number. If you're working on your research and have any questions or doubts, by all means, reach out to me. It would be a pleasure to help you." He handed me a card and I took it, placing it in my purse without reading it.

"Thank you so much. That's… very nice of you." I was taken completely by surprise.

He gave me that faint smile of his, bowed, and walked back to the restaurant. I got into my car and drove home, fantasizing about inviting him to my place to talk about Greece and… who was I kidding? I drove home fantasizing about kissing him and making passionate love to him. It was really the craziest thing ever. I had never ever felt so smitten by someone like this before. Was I bewitched? I was being ridiculous. He was obviously just interested in showing off his knowledge, his expertise, and sharing his beautiful and rich culture with a student. Like he said, *"that's what motivates the teacher, you know…"*

When I got home, I tried to work on my paper, but I couldn't focus on it. Why did I have to pick as my subject the damned Greek bronze vessels to do my final paper on? Everything about Greece only reminded me of Nikos, his voice, his eyes, his body. It was such an irrational feeling, but I couldn't control the absurd attraction I felt for this man, like a magnet. I wondered if every other woman who had met him was thinking the same. And the hunk of my wildest dreams was Maggie's lover.

Chapter 4

The following week proved to be very busy. I met everyone who worked in the Arts of Africa, Oceania, and the Americas' curatorial department, and had plenty of work to do. The department's main goal for the summer was to expand and redesign the African galleries, which was going to be a robust project. After all, the collection featured masks, sculptures, headdresses, textiles and objects from a variety of regions, cultures, and countries from 500 BC to the present. Some gold masterpieces would require extensive care and handling expertise. I was glad I was going to be involved in such a detailed project, so I would have less time to fantasize about Nikos, and would be busy with work I really enjoyed doing. A few days after we met at Theo's Jane invited me for lunch after a hectic morning. We hadn't seen each other since that evening. We sat by the bar.

"I'm so busy in my department. It's a wonderful project we're working on."

"Me too," Jane responded. "We barely have time to go to the restroom. Have you gotten word from Dr. Jones about working with Nikos yet?"

"Not a word. I'm not going to insist on it. I understand he's very busy and then, there's Maggie, his body guard," I teased.

Jane laughed heartily. "That's what she looks like when she's around him. I still can't quite figure out how she ended up meeting him earlier than everyone else. She's already dating the man and he's been here less than two weeks."

"It's a shame, I'd really love to hear what he has to say about the vessels and all, but I understand."

"What did he tell you when he walked you to your car that evening? You know, Maggie was fuming. She almost had a heart attack when he followed you. I could see it in her eyes, but she didn't say anything to him when he got back to the table."

"Well… he just wanted to tell me he would love to help me out with my project. He gave me his card if I ever needed help with my research."

"Are you serious? He gave you his number? Then, call him! What are you waiting for? Maybe he wants you to call him."

"Don't be crazy, Jane. He told me that an interested student like me is what motivates a teacher like him. He's dating Maggie and I don't want any issues with that woman. You know how loud she can be when she thinks someone is after one of her boyfriends? Remember that incident a few months ago when she was dating the student from the Engineering department and thought the girl who worked at the library was flirting with him?"

"She's loud and obnoxious, yes, and I don't know why she's so insecure and so jealous. She's gorgeous and rich. But this time she got herself a real god. This guy is too perfect to be true. Don't you feel almost intimidated in his presence?"

Intimidated. That's the word I had been looking for to describe how I felt in Nikos' presence. And I had seen this man only twice. He was definitely intimidating in a sexy, sensual way.

"Yes. He is intimidating. I can't quite figure out why."

"He's way too good looking, very smart, and he has an aura about him, I think," Jane said. "I'm sure almost every woman in the department is in love with him."

"You think so?"

"I don't mean literally, but I've seen the looks of other women when they see him. And I haven't even been around him that much. Maggie is going to have a hard time keeping prying eyes away from him," Jane said. "You, for instance."

"Me?" I asked, quite perplexed.

"Sabrina, we've been friends for a long time. I can tell when you're uncomfortable in someone's presence. And his presence has a disturbing effect on you."

"Don't be ridiculous. I don't even know him… Besides, he's dating Maggie."

"It doesn't matter. You can't hide it from me. You're not quite yourself in his presence."

19

"Do you really know me so well, or is it that visible? Please, Jane, don't tease me about it. I don't know why I just fell head over heels for a guy I've seen only twice… It's totally embarrassing."

"Chill out, girl," Jane said. "He's really handsome and intelligent and… well, as far as we can tell, he's a perfect Greek god. I don't know what he sees in Maggie, though. She's a beautiful woman, but I just can't picture them together as a couple. It doesn't click. It looks like she has him under a leash although he doesn't seem to be that much into her."

"I can't take him out of my mind, Jane. It's like an obsession. I'm even afraid of my feelings."

"I hope Dr. Jones arranges something for you two to get to know each other better."

"Ha-ha-ha," I laughed. "If he only knew how I feel. And to know each other better? Yeah, I wish! There's no time for it. He's only here for two months."

"Too bad, isn't it? Well, let's go back to work. Let me know as soon as you get word from Dr. Jones about your session with Nikos. I can't wait to see Maggie's face."

Even though I had tried to disguise my emotions, it was discomforting to know my demeanor in Nikos' presence was so evident. At least it was for Jane, so I wondered if Maggie had also noticed the way I melted whenever he was around. She didn't know me that well, and I hadn't been around Nikos much, so hopefully it was not an issue. Yet. Everyone knew Maggie wasn't the smartest cookie in school, but she was very popular not only because of her beauty, but her father. Mr. Wallendorf was an art collector, a rich investor, and a huge benefactor of the museum.

When I got back to the African art gallery, I couldn't believe my eyes. Nikos was there, like a vision - a god from Olympus. I slowed my pace. He looked absolutely stunning, dressed in a black polo shirt and beige Dockers, his hands inside his pockets while he talked to one of the curators. I was enjoying his muscular physique from a distance, at least for the few minutes before he noticed me walking into the gallery. What was he doing in my department? When he saw me coming, he bowed and greeted me with a husky and sexy voice, which almost made me blush.

"Hello. It's nice to see you again. How is your project on the Greek vessels coming along?"

I stared at him for a second before I came back to earth to answer.

"Oh, the project... I haven't had the time to devote to it recently. I've been busy with my work here, redesigning this gallery," I lied. I couldn't focus on working with anything that reminded me of him. I couldn't get him off my mind.

"It's a demanding assignment, that's for sure. I hope you're enjoying it."

"Yes, I'm learning a lot. Thank you. Are you interested in African art?"

"As an archaeologist, I can say I'm always curious about everything that has been unearthed and placed in a museum. I have worked in excavations both in Egypt and sub-Saharan Africa."

"It must have been fascinating to travel to those places and dig. Are you looking for any specific item in the collection that I can show you?"

"I'm looking for you, actually," he said.

I tilted my head in surprise, while my heart quickened. "For me?"

"Yes. I wanted to tell you that if you're still interested in my assistance, Dr. Jones and I are almost done finalizing a plan to schedule you to visit with me for an afternoon next week."

My heart pounded faster. Spending a whole afternoon with him talking about Greek art. What could I say not to sound so anxious?

"I'd... love that. I'll definitely work on my project during the weekend, so I'll come prepared with questions, if you don't mind."

"I don't mind at all. I'm looking forward to discussing it with you," he said, and for a minute I thought he stared at me with

21

renewed intensity. I brushed it off; it could only be my imagination. He was certainly just looking forward to showing off his scholarly knowledge.

"There you are again. You keep running off! I have to introduce you at your next lecture, Nikos, and it's starting in… like… five minutes!" Maggie burst into the gallery, walking straight towards us in a fast pace.

Nikos looked at his watch. "I'm sorry; I'm almost late for my lecture. I'll see you later."

He walked away from me and met Maggie half way. She touched his arm in that same possessive manner and started rushing him out of the gallery. Before exiting, she looked back and glanced at me from head to toe. How could he let this woman dominate him like that? She seemed to really have him on a leash, like Jane said. Wherever Nikos was, she always found him and whisked him away. Did she have a special GPS wired to him? How unnerving. I had to contain the foolish desire I had for this man. It was growing in intensity every time I saw him, and soon it would become too apparent that I was drooling for him. The way Maggie looked back at me was disconcerting. She would think I was after her boyfriend and the last thing I wanted was a confrontation with her about someone I didn't even know. How upsetting that would be.

I kept myself busy to avoid thinking about my Greek obsession until it was time to go home. When I got to the car, I realized I had turned my cell phone off and had not checked it even once during the whole day. Dr. Jones had left me a message. He was able to fit me in to work with Dr. Soulis the following Monday afternoon. He ended the message recommending for me to take ample advantage of the opportunity, because it was going to be a one on one session. He asked me to call him back to confirm I was in agreement with the plan. What was I going to do? Although I desperately wanted it, it was going to be painful to spend the whole afternoon with Nikos talking about Greek vases. I had to control my lust for him. All I wanted was for him to hold me in his arms, kiss me and make passionate love to me. Why did I have to fall for him? I thought about calling Dr. Jones to cancel the arrangement, but I called Jane instead.

"I need your advice. Bad."

"Shoot it."

"Dr. Jones called me. I have a whole afternoon with Nikos next Monday."

"Wow! Great news!" Jane said. "And… what do you want my advice for…?"

"I'm thinking of giving an excuse. I can't go. I'm head over heels for this guy. He was looking for me today at the African arts department."

"He was looking for you? Jeez, Sabrina, you're in trouble."

"No, not that way, Jane, no. He was looking for me to tell me they were working something out for next week. It was before Dr. Jones left me a message. He is looking for an interested student and I'm it."

"But you can't pass this opportunity. You have to be reasonable. Besides, it would be very rude for you not to accept. It seems they went to great lengths to change his schedule and fit you in."

"Yes, you're right. I don't think I can get away from it. How can I quench my desire for him, though? I can't shake him out of my mind, I'm really obsessed. Oh, and Maggie saw us talking."

"Are you serious? Did she say anything?"

"She came looking for him, as usual, and found us talking in the African art gallery. He walked away before she got too close, but she gave me a nasty look. She has him on a leash, Jane, like you said. It's almost painful to see how he sort of does whatever she says."

"What was her excuse this time?"

"Apparently he was about to give a lecture and she was going to introduce him," I said.

"Call Dr. Jones right away and confirm. Let's hope Maggie won't show up for your one on one afternoon session. I know it will be hard, but try to study this weekend and put down on paper as much as you want to know about the subject. I'd hate for you to screw up this golden opportunity."

"I know. You're right. I have to keep my head on my shoulders and be sensible about it. Just because I'm infatuated with the man, I can't throw away this chance to learn something that will help me with my research and future career."

I called Dr. Jones and left him a message thanking him and Dr. Soulis for the opportunity, and stressing how much I was looking forward to Monday afternoon. I wondered what had been canceled in Nikos' schedule for them to fit me in. For my sake and for Nikos' willingness to work with me, I had to make it worthwhile. By the week's end, I hadn't heard anything else about Nikos, which was better for my sanity. I had to focus on studying during the weekend, focus on taking Nikos out of my mind, and make sure I had enough material to cover for a whole afternoon with him.

On Sunday evening, Jane called to check on me.

"I spent the whole weekend writing the paper and researching about the Greek vessels, Jane. I'm really putting all my heart into it. I don't want to make a fool of myself in front of Nikos tomorrow. Can you imagine how embarrassing if he considered the time spent with me and my project unproductive?"

"I'm glad you were able to focus. You have to behave professionally and try to disguise your lust for him."

"That's the hard part. But I'll manage. Thanks for your support, girlfriend."

I tried to go to bed early to be well rested and refreshed to start the week, but I had no luck. My mind was playing tricks on me. Whenever I closed my eyes all I saw was Nikos' perfectly tanned and well-built figure, sporting his to die-for-smile. Why was I so helplessly infatuated with this man? I'd been in love before, or so I thought at the time, but nothing remotely close to what I felt for Nikos. I had broken up with my last boyfriend nearly four months ago. We didn't have much in common and just started drifting apart. Steve was adorable when we began dating, but a few weeks into our relationship, I realized he was too much of a jock for my taste. Instead of inviting me out to the movies, or to a concert, or to anything romantic like the opera or ballet, which was my idea of a great date, his idea of a great date was in the ballpark. After I attended a few sporting events with him, I figured I was wasting my time; we had no common interests. He didn't appreciate my love for the arts and I didn't appreciate his love for sports either, to his sheer disappointment. He hadn't gotten over me completely, every once in a while he would still call me and invite me out, but I wasn't inclined to give him another chance.

****

The museum was closed. The long, white marble halls were filled with the silence of timeless works of art and stone figures staring at us. I was a helpless nymph, half naked lying on the red silk covered divan, subdued by the powerfully seductive god. The bare-chested Olympian poured fragrant oil all over my breasts. He started slowly, rubbing, massaging, teasing, rolling and raising my nipples in-between his strong, massive fingers until they were as big and hard as two pink pearls. Satisfied with their firmness, he made his way along my body with both his manly hands, leisurely caressing my chest and navel all the way down to my groin. He delicately opened my legs and spread them apart, and I surrendered myself completely to his will. He rubbed the oil on my most sensitive area, fierce in his tease, inducing fragrant moisture from within me. With my sexual tension building up, the handsome Greek god held me captive and moved on to rub and massage my legs, calves, ankles, feet and toes. I gasped in ecstasy when he started sucking the flavorful oil from my toes. While I groaned and moaned in delightful abandon, his wet tongue and soft lips moved up my legs until he was face to face with my moistness. He eagerly licked the oil mixed with my juice, working his tongue back and forth, in and out, lavishing in my movements as I raised my hips and body in anticipation of my inevitable orgasm. He licked, bit and sucked all corners of me until he heard the release of my ultimate scream. A larger than life bronze Poseidon watched me, seemingly oblivious to my pleasure.

I woke up shuddering, feeling feverish. Although I had finally fallen asleep, my subconscious mind kept Nikos alive, too alive, indeed.

Chapter 5

After last night's erotic dream, I regretted having agreed to a study session with Nikos. I had no idea how I was going to control my growing desire for the man I was spending the whole afternoon with. I needed to cool off and talk to someone, so I sent Jane a text early in the morning inviting her to have lunch with me before meeting Nikos.

As soon as I arrived in the museum, I walked straight to my department and worked furiously on an African gold mask display until it was time to go to lunch. The more I kept busy, the less I had time to fantasize about Nikos and remember the sexy dream. Jane was already waiting for me inside the restaurant.

"I have no idea what I got myself into," I said as soon as I saw her.

"What happened now? Was your meeting canceled or rescheduled?"

"No, unfortunately, no. Jane, I had the most erotic dream last night. Nikos was an Olympian god and I was a nymph, and we were right here in the museum, and oh… it was hot!"

"Oh, my. Now you're going to meet your Zeus in real life."

"What am I going to do? I'm going crazy because of this dream. It sounds ludicrous, but I felt as if the dream was true and he knows about it."

"It felt that real, huh? That's insane. The Greek charmer really got to you. I don't know what to tell you," Jane said, shaking her head. "My advice is for you to bring your notes and whatever material you have, keep your eyes on your research paper, and avoid looking at him at all costs. Pretend it is Dr. Jones you're talking to, not the Greek god."

"Yeah, I'll try that. Please wish me luck so I don't make a fool of myself in front of him. I'm embarrassed enough already."

"Don't drool over your papers," Jane teased. I looked at her, shook my head and smiled. I had to keep calm, and be ready to meet the god who had massaged my body with hot oil and

27

licked me all over last night, giving me the best imagined climax ever. It felt so real I could still feel my body quivering from the long lasting orgasmic sensation.

As soon as we were done with lunch, I walked into the restroom to brush my teeth and recompose myself. I applied a dab of perfume behind my ears, combed my hair, took a deep breath, put some light pink lipstick on just to give my face a little color, and topped it off with a clear lip gloss. I was ready to slay the dragon. The door to the conference room was open. Nikos was inside adjusting a laptop to make sure it was connected to the projector, and he didn't seem to notice me as I came in. Wearing a pair of jeans and a plain gray T-shirt highlighting his square shoulders and strong, bronzed arms, his disheveled black hair gave him a casual look – the stereotype of a Hollywood field archaeologist. Indiana Jones meets Odysseus.

"Good afternoon. I hope I'm on time," I said shyly.

He looked up with his hypnotizing eyes and bowed at me courteously.

"I'm glad you could make it. I have a couple of things planned for our session. But you're welcome to interrupt me and change directions if I'm not touching on a specific topic you need more insight into," he said, gesturing for me to take a seat.

"You prepared an agenda?" I asked while sitting down and placing my research papers and folder on the table.

"I like to keep things organized. I have several photos I'd like to show you of my excavations on a site in Greece where my team found objects dating to the same period several of the bronze vessels in the collection are from. These objects will give you an idea of how life was – or was supposed to be, in the eighth or ninth centuries B.C."

"Wow, that's really amazing. I find it fascinating that you've participated in real excavations and I'd love to see it," I said. He sounded excited about showing me his pictures and clicked on the laptop. The screen lit up with an image of archaeologist Nikos in action. In the photo, he was squatting next to a hole

28

on the floor and holding what looked like a piece of earthenware, his eyes squinting from the sun shining on his face. He was wearing a plain white T-shirt and a pair of cargo shorts, allowing a view of his tanned legs. This afternoon was going to be worse than I could possibly imagine. How would I keep from drooling?

"I'm sorry. I don't want to impose an agenda on you. Please tell me what you have done so far in your project, how you're coming along in your research, and we can go from there."

I snapped out of my daze as soon as I heard him. "Oh, please, continue. I'd love to see the pictures of the excavation and I'll be taking notes. I can show you where I am on my work when we finish looking at them."

"Do you have any questions before I start?" he asked.

"Do you prefer your work in the field as an archaeologist? Is it what gives you more satisfaction in this line of work? I mean, it's just… well, you seem to be so proud of it."

He gave me a faint smile and sat down opposite from me. "Looking for an archaeological treasure, or a piece of evidence from a remote past, is like a game of seduction," he said, keeping his eyes on me like a laser beam. "I love the chase. Researching the object you want to conquer, longing to touch it, to feel it, to breathe it, to know everything about it." He paused, looking deep into my eyes. I froze, imagining myself as the object of his lust, the relic he wanted to find, to touch, to feel. "You dig, excavate, think you're close to it and it eludes you. The hunt takes over your senses, you become obsessed and all you think about is the thrill of finally possessing it. And when you finally find it, all the tension is released… like an indulgent pleasure."

I let out a soft gasp. His seductive description of a dig turned me on even more than I already was. Was he intentionally doing it? Could he sense my rising hormones every time I was in his presence? Was he a dream or a reality? He was a charmer and Jane was right, he was getting the best of me.

"Should we start, or do you have any other questions?" he asked, awakening me once more from a semi-coma state. I managed to blink my eyes.

"Yes, please, start," was all that came out in a barely audible voice.

Nikos clicked on the laptop to reveal more provocative pictures of him in the archaeological site. He paused in each picture to explain where it was taken and what he had found, and I tried to take notes to avoid looking at him with longing eyes. After the last image, he closed down the laptop and looked at me. "Any questions about this presentation on archaeological findings?"

I finished writing down something about the last photo, which showed the remnants of a temple column. I didn't know what to ask. I felt as if he could read my mind, as if he knew I was fantasizing about him. "No, you've done a great job explaining each picture, and I took enough notes. This will help me elaborate on the lifestyle of the ancient Greeks who used those vessels. Thank you so much."

He got up from his chair and approached me. Standing next to me, emanating a slight musky, masculine scent, he picked up the folder I had placed on the table. "Do you mind if I take a look?"

"Please do so. I would love your feedback," I said, drinking in his delicious scent. He pulled the chair next to me and sat down unceremoniously, leafing through my research paper with attention. I couldn't help staring at his expression. He didn't seem to notice I was intently looking at him, and continued to go through the material for a few minutes in silence.

"Is it that bad?" I asked, since he had not made any comments yet about my work.

He was startled by my interruption. "No, not really. On the contrary, so far it looks good. You're doing a thorough research. It's actually better than I anticipated."

Better than he anticipated? What kind of opinion did he have of me? His comment caught me off guard. Was he thinking I was a lousy student who didn't know how to write a proper research paper? I didn't know whether to feel offended or not. He must have noticed the strange look on my face - I really felt like he was reading my mind.

30

"I didn't mean it in a bad way. I'm surprised you know so much about a subject that doesn't drive enough interest among most students. May I ask why you chose this topic?"

"Thank you... I'm flattered to know you like my research so far. I chose it because I haven't come across many academic publications about these vessels. I've always been fascinated by Greek culture and archeology. When I see a Greek vase, it tells me a story, always portraying scenes of everyday life. It is amazing how each image shows so much documentation about Greek mythological and religious beliefs. And when I found out the museum was hosting a special exhibit on the Greek vessels, I jumped at the chance to do more research on it." He placed my papers back on the table and got up from the chair.

"Yes, the images reproduced in the vases can transport us directly to the worlds of Homer, Pericles, Sophocles, Alexander the Great... an amazing time period," he said pensively. "Should we go take a look at the vases? You can show me what you know about them."

We left the conference room and rode the escalator to the second floor, where the Greek Bronze Vessels exhibit was being shown. It was Monday and since the museum was closed to the public, we were the only ones in the empty gallery, which reminded of my dream. We walked silently to the first vase and stopped. Nikos asked me to describe it to him. I examined the piece without looking at the name plate placed at the base of the glass case where the vase was enclosed. If he was genuinely impressed with my research paper, I wanted to astonish him with my knowledge. I gave him a brief description of the piece, and tried to elaborate on its usage and importance. I faced him but couldn't quite read his expression. He bowed his head the way he often did, and gave me his faint smile again. We moved on to the next object, and I repeated the exercise every time we stopped to look at one of them. He was silent, carefully observing me and listening to what I had to say about each vessel. When we got to a smaller vase, I hesitated. I hadn't done enough research on what appeared to be a more feminine type of container.

31

"This is a different type of vase. It was usually found in the women's quarters. It is a geometric bronze pyxis," he said, noticing my uncertainty.

"Oh… a pyxis? What is it?"

"A pyxis is an antique type of cylindrical box with a lid. The women often used this type of small vessel to keep jewelry, cosmetics, and sometimes perfume," Nikos explained. "By the way," he continued, "what perfume are you wearing? It's an intoxicating fragrance."

What perfume was I wearing? Did I hear that right? I had dabbed just a few drops behind my ears after lunch and I had no idea the scent was emanating so strongly for him to notice it. I looked at him perplexed by his question. Again, as if reading my facial expression, or my mind, he spoke before I could answer him.

"I'm so sorry. It's not my place to invade your privacy asking you personal questions like that. I didn't mean to make you uncomfortable. Let's move on. Do you have any questions about the pyxis?"

Oh, the tease. He asked me a personal question, finally, and then he didn't let me answer it. What was he trying to do to me? I was totally taken by this man. There was no need for more seduction.

"Is this the only pyxis in the collection?" I tried to pretend his previous question hadn't affected me. "I'd like to learn more about the women's vessels to incorporate them into my research. I think it will be a nice touch to include them as well. I was focusing on the larger vessels."

"Excellent idea. We will talk more about it when we go back to the conference room. Let's continue."

"*Chance*." I whispered.

"Chance?" He faced me, obviously confused by what I had just mumbled.

"The name of my perfume. It's *Chance* by Chanel." I knew I was blushing.

He smiled at me as if acknowledging my answer but didn't say anything and we continued walking. How I wanted to be taken by him just like in my dream.

As we passed in front of the break room, Nikos paused for a minute. "Would you like to have a cup of coffee before going back to the conference room?" he asked. I nodded in agreement. We sat at a table in the back of the break room after helping ourselves to a cup of coffee. I was feeling anxious; I didn't know what was coming next. Having coffee was a break from the study atmosphere and it might give us room for some more personal interaction.

"I'm very impressed with your knowledge of the Greek culture," Nikos started. "I've never met a student who has been so engrossed in this subject before. Thank you."

"I'm the one who must thank you. Your feedback and teaching has been invaluable so far. It will greatly help me with my paper. I can't thank you enough for your time in doing this. I'm sorry you had to cancel another appointment to fit me into your busy schedule."

"It's my pleasure. Dr. Jones hadn't realized my activity this afternoon was actually a tour of the theater district with one of the docent volunteers. Basically, it was a free afternoon for me to visit the city. I can do that another time."

"I'm sorry I'm interfering with your time off," I apologized again.

"Talking to you about Greek art is much better than a boring afternoon visiting the theater district. I'd rather attend a performance than visit the area on a Monday afternoon. I'm a big fan of the ballet."

"Really? I love it too," I said, surprised by his revelation.

"My mother was a ballerina. I used to see her perform when I was a little kid, and took a liking for the music and the dance," Nikos said. "It would be nice to see a performance here if I had the time and company."

"I… I can take you to the ballet on Saturday if you'd like. It's the last weekend they're performing *The Swan Lake* and it's one of my favorites. Would you like to go?" I couldn't believe what I had just said. I was inviting Nikos to go out to the ballet with me. Did I go crazy? Wasn't he dating Maggie?

"I'm sure you have better plans for Saturday night than to escort a foreign visitor to the ballet. I'd hate to burden you with that."

"It's not a burden at all. I have no plans for this Saturday night, and it would be my pleasure to escort you to the performance. Consider it my thank you for being so generous with me today." Nikos took a sip of his coffee and gazed at me without saying a word, as if he was pondering the pros and cons of my invitation. I looked at him, eagerly waiting for an answer. After a few minutes, he spoke almost as if in a whisper, his voice coming out huskier and sexier than normal.

"I'd love to. I'll get back with you later to confirm."

I nodded at him and smiled nervously. We finished our coffee, left the break room, and walked back to the conference room where I wrote down information about the interesting pyxis he had explained to me during our tour of the exhibit. I thought I had enough material to elaborate further on my paper, and felt good about it. It had been a rewarding afternoon. And the prospect of going to the ballet with Nikos on Saturday night would definitely end the week on a special note. It was nearing 5 p.m., so I got ready to go.

"Are you working longer today?" I asked him.

"No. I'm done here if you don't have any further questions. Remember, it was supposed to be my free afternoon," he joked.

I smiled. "Are you staying somewhere close to the museum?"

"Yes, I rented a furnished apartment close by. I have to wait for my ride, though." As soon as he said that, Maggie came bursting through the door. She looked as if she was in a hurry but stopped suddenly when she realized I was in there with Nikos, and stared at me from head to toe.

"I'm glad I'm not running late. I thought you were giving a lecture here," she said, taking her eyes off me and facing Nikos.

"You're right on time, Maggie. Thanks. We've just finished," Nikos responded.

"Where are the other students… is everyone already gone?" she asked.

"She's the student," Nikos said, turning to me.

"Hello, Maggie," I said.

She glanced at me with a puzzled expression, ignoring my greeting. "She's the only one?"

"Yes, we had a great session today. Time very well spent. It's great when a student is interested in learning," Nikos said.

I could sense Maggie's jealousy. Apparently, she didn't know I was the only student he had been lecturing that afternoon. I was in an uncomfortable situation. He was stating, as a matter-of-fact, what I represented to him: an interested student. Hadn't he been flirting with me? Was I misinterpreting something? I was a fool. Nikos and Maggie were definitely a couple and I was his student. There was nothing else to it. I wanted to tell him to forget about my invitation to go to the ballet, but of course I didn't want to mention anything about it in front of Maggie. It was better for me to leave, and hope he would refuse the invitation.

"Again, thank you for your help. I really appreciate your time teaching me about the Greek vessels," I said, getting ready to leave.

Nikos smiled. "It was my pleasure. I'll get back to you later and please don't hesitate to contact me if you have any questions while going over the material or while writing your paper."

"See you later, Maggie," I turned to her before leaving the room. She gave me a forced smile before rolling her eyes.

How jealous I was of Maggie. I wish I could give Nikos a ride and take him to his place. Maybe I was being naïve, but I'm sure I felt a strong sexual tension between Nikos and me during our afternoon session. He had asked me about my perfume before taking it back as an inappropriate question. When we were having coffee and talked about ballet, he sounded interested in my invitation, although he didn't accept it right away. Was I really seeing things where there was nothing to be seen? I didn't care. I was more and more captivated by him and I wasn't going to avoid him because he was dating Maggie. He was in town for only two months and if I had the chance of spending any time with the irresistible, sexy, intelligent, and handsome god of my dreams, I would. All I had so far was a dream, and that couldn't hurt me.

Chapter 6

The week was going by as planned, especially since I was overwhelmed with the redesigning of my department and didn't want to let Nikos' presence interfere with my work. I knew he was busier than I was, and I hadn't seen him since Monday afternoon. I told Jane all the details about our study session, except for my bold move inviting Nikos to the ballet. I hadn't heard from him yet, so I kept this piece of information to myself. I was sure he was not going to accept. Wouldn't he rather go to the ballet with his girlfriend Maggie instead of me? Nikos was being discreet about his relationship with her and had never mentioned anything about it, even though he had the opportunity to do so. I didn't notice him looking at her with loving longing eyes when she came to pick him up Monday afternoon, but that's what I wanted to believe. However, she guarded him like a bodyguard, and she was aware of his every step.

On Thursday morning, I went down to the storage room to retrieve a particular object we were rebuilding a display for when I ran into Maggie on my way back to the African art gallery.

"Sabrina, can I have a word with you?" she asked when she saw me.

"Hello, Maggie. Are you enjoying your work as a docent volunteer?"

"I don't have time for small talk with you, Sabrina. I want to know what it is that Nikos needs to get back to you about."

I was taken completely by surprise. No wonder Maggie really had a reputation for being a bitch whenever she was dating someone. "What are you talking about?"

"The other day when I picked him up, he told you he was going to get back with you. What was that about?" she insisted.

"My research paper. What is the problem with you? Nikos is helping me out with my research paper, you know that."

"I know your excuse, asking him to help you with school work. Back off, Sabrina. Nikos is with me, and I don't appreciate you trying to waste his time," she said curtly.

"I don't need to give you any explanation about my relationship with Nikos or what we discussed. He's a grown man. If he didn't want to teach me, he wouldn't have allocated his time to do so."

"I'm warning you to back off. I better not see you around him anymore. You already had your study session with him. That's enough."

"I'm not after your *boyfriend*, Maggie. But if I need his help with my paper, I won't hesitate to ask for his assistance. He is a respected professional and we can all benefit from his expertise while he's here." I walked away without giving her a chance to reply.

I couldn't believe she had the guts to confront me about him. She was unnerving. Now what? What if Nikos accepted my invitation to go to the ballet Saturday night? Should I allow myself to be scared by this woman? She was behaving in a very insecure way and I wondered if she was approaching every other woman who had attended one of Nikos' lectures or classes, or spent any time talking to him, to warn them to back off. Or was it just me? I didn't want any problems with Maggie, but I wasn't going to let myself be intimidated like that. I wasn't going to stop talking to him or enjoying his presence because of her bouts of jealousy. She would have to deal with it or get over it. Obviously, Nikos was referring to the ballet when he told me he was going to get back with me, but if she hadn't gotten that information from him, she wouldn't get it from me either.

I was carefully cleaning the ceremonial gold mask I had retrieved from the storage room when the curator approached me to let me know there was a call for me in her office. I checked my cell phone to see if I had accidentally turned it off or if there was a missed call, but that was not the case. I walked to the curator's office and picked up the receiver.

"This is Sabrina."

"Hello, Sabrina. Nikos here. I'm sorry to bother you, but I don't have your cell phone."

My heart almost stopped beating. The object of my forbidden desire was on the other line, looking for me.

"Hello, Nikos," I muttered, trying to disguise my excitement.

"I was hoping to walk to your gallery and talk to you in person, but I'm really busy. I wanted to let you know, if it's not too late and if your invitation still stands, that I'd very much like to go to the ballet on Saturday night."

"Are you sure you want me to escort you? I mean, you really don't have someone you'd rather go with?" I could hear my heart pounding. Wouldn't you rather go with Maggie, your bodyguard? I wanted to ask him but I didn't dare.

"Of course I'm sure. I'm sorry it took me a few days to get back with you. I wanted to check with Dr. Jones about any policies in regards to interactions with museum personnel. I'm not used to going out with students and I don't want you to get in trouble during your internship because of me."

Oh. He is not used to going out with students? Evidently, Maggie is not "his" student. She's a museum volunteer, that's it. What a big difference. I needed to get over it. I was just a student, and Maggie was his girlfriend. And for some unknown reason he was not going to the ballet with his girlfriend, but with a student. After the confrontation with Maggie this morning, the whole situation seemed too cumbersome. But it was too late for me to back off. And why should I care? After all, I was going to watch my favorite ballet with a handsome Greek god who inhabited my most secret dreams. But I had to put myself in my place - I was his student.

"OK." I said.

"Give me your cell number. I'm on my way to a meeting but I want to give you a call later to talk about Saturday."

I gave him my cell number and he hung up. I was almost sure he was not going to accept my invitation, and to my utter surprise, he did. But I was confused about his relationship with Maggie and wondered why he wouldn't go out with her on a Saturday night. My mind started working on plausible explanations. Did she confront him about me and they got into a fight? Or maybe she didn't like to go to the ballet. No, she wouldn't leave him alone on a Saturday night if she was that jealous of him. Something must have happened between them. Or was it just a coincidence that she came to talk to me this morning about backing off and then he called me in the afternoon to accept my invitation? Immersed in these thoughts, I walked back to the gallery.

"Is everything OK?" The curator asked me when she saw me coming back.

"Yes, thank you. Someone was trying to reach me but didn't have my cell number. Thank you again," I said before resuming my work on the African gold mask.

By the time I left the museum that afternoon, I hadn't heard from Nikos again. As soon as I arrived home, I logged on the computer to search for seats for Saturday night's performance. While I was searching, my cell rang. I felt my heartbeat skipping faster.

"Hello?"

"Hello, Sabrina." I heard the sexiest voice ever on the other side. Oh, my, what was this man doing to me? Was this really love at first sight?

"Hi, Nikos," I said. "I was looking for tickets for Saturday, and there are still some really nice seats available."

"I'm glad to hear that. I'm looking forward to this performance. What time do you want to meet?"

"What about I pick you up at seven? The performance starts at eight. That should give us plenty of time to get to our seats without rushing," I suggested.

"Sounds good. Write down my address. I will be waiting for you downstairs by the gate, so you won't have to bother calling in." Nikos spelled his address out for me.

"Got it. I'll be there at seven then."

"Sabrina, I need to ask you one thing, please."

"Yes?"

"Please keep this to yourself. As I told you before, it's against my personal policy going out with students and colleagues, and I prefer we remain diplomatic about it. If you don't mind."

He was really trying to keep it under the radar. Was it because of Maggie? Or was he embarrassed about going out with a student? What was the real problem? I didn't know what to say.

"Are you OK with it?" Nikos insisted, sensing my silence.

"If this is such an important issue for you, shouldn't we cancel it if it makes you so... uncomfortable?" I asked.

"I want to go to the ballet with you. I'm making an exception, but I prefer to be discreet about my personal life outside of work. I don't mean to upset you, but I'd rather keep it just between the two of us. Please." I sighed. He still didn't mention anything about his relationship with Maggie. I wanted to ask him about it, but it was better not to intrude.

"Yes, sure, no problem then. Whatever works best for you. I'll be discreet about it, don't worry," I said somewhat disappointed.

"Thank you so much. I'm looking forward to Saturday."

"Me too," I whispered before he hung up.

I closed my eyes, trying to shake away an awkward feeling. I wasn't going to tell Jane about my upcoming "date" with Nikos which was, in fact, not a date but a student escorting a professor to the ballet. And the professor didn't want anyone knowing the student was escorting him. Why didn't he just tell me he was dating Maggie and didn't want her to find out? He was finding an excuse by telling me about his personal policy of not going out with students or colleagues for the sake of his relationship with her. I felt like calling him back to confront him about it, but that would be ridiculous of me. I shouldn't let him know how much I disliked this situation and how much I wanted to know what was the real deal between them, so I

41

decided to go on with his request. At least, he was making an exception for me.

Chapter 7

I was getting dressed to go pick up my Olympian god for our big fake date. What should I wear? I tried on several dresses, skirts, blouses, shoes, and I still couldn't figure out what would be appropriate. As if Nikos would notice. I had to be realistic and remember: he made an exception and allowed me to be his escort for the ballet because he wanted to attend the performance, not because he wanted to enjoy the evening with *me*. Don't be silly, Sabrina. Act your part, you're the student – I told myself. But my yearning to smell his scent, to enjoy his presence, and to hear his hushed voice excited me beyond words. I finally settled for a light blue chiffon cocktail dress with a navy blue shawl, since it would be chilly inside the theater, and matching navy blue sexy high heeled dress shoes. I wore my long brown hair straight, applied light make up, and didn't forget to dab some *Chance* perfume at the back of my wrists and ears, and on my cleavage, hoping Nikos would notice it. I looked at myself in the mirror and liked what I saw. I looked classy, elegant, not like an average student escorting her professor to an event, so I grabbed my navy blue clutch bag and walked to the parking garage.

A Herculean vision stood by the gate at the luxury apartment complex. Dressed in a three piece light brown suit, my Olympian looked like a fashionable and stylish model from The Rake or Man of the World magazines, wearing a nice pair of aviator sunglasses with his hands in his pockets, waiting for me. I drove closer to the gate, rolled down the window and waved at him. He walked up to my car, opened the passenger's door and sat next to me.

"I hope you haven't been waiting long," I said.

"Perfect timing," he replied, handing me an envelope. I looked at him questioningly. "This is to cover the tickets for tonight's performance."

"You… no, that's not necessary. This is my gift to you, my thank you for spending an afternoon helping me with my project, please," I protested.

"You don't need to thank me, Sabrina. It was my pleasure teaching you. I spent a very enjoyable afternoon with you and there's no need for you to pay me back," Nikos said in a serious tone. "And I'm sure we will have a lovely evening. Please." He insisted. I took the envelope and stuffed it inside my clutch bag.

"Please don't feel offended. I wouldn't feel comfortable knowing you're taking me out to thank me for my job. I love teaching what I know and you're a great student," he said. Oh, my Greek hero, do you have to remind me so often I'm just a student to you?

"I'm sorry. I didn't mean to make you uncomfortable, I just..." I didn't know what to say and I was afraid to spoil the mood.

"You just...?" he questioned when I didn't complete my sentence.

"I just wanted to make sure you knew how much I appreciate the time you spent with me." He took his sunglasses off and stared at me.

"I know." I felt a jolt of electricity throughout my body and had to restrain myself from not tilting my head to kiss him passionately on his lips. I lowered my eyes to avoid his stare and turned the key in the ignition.

"We better go, so we can find a good parking spot," I said as I drove off.

It was a short drive from the Museum District apartment, where he was staying, to the Wortham Theater downtown. We were relatively early, so I found a good parking spot with ease, and we climbed the stairs to the theater's foyer. I walked up to the "will call" window, retrieved the tickets and handed them to the attendant, who showed us the way to the level where our orchestra seats were located.

"Would you like a glass of wine before we take our seats?" Nikos asked, breaking the silence. We were about 30 minutes early, and there was enough time for a drink at the theater's bar.

"Sure." We walked up to the bar and Nikos ordered two glasses of white wine. He handed me a glass and cheered.

"To a delightful evening," he said. I smiled and took a sip of the delicious wine. I really needed a drink to relax. Being next to Nikos was nerve-wrecking; my emotions were all over the place. My desire for this man was such that it paralyzed me.

"And I forgot to mention, you look stunning. Blue is my favorite color."

I took two more sips of the wine. "Thank you." I knew I was blushing, so I looked away from him, feasting my eyes on the colorful array of elegantly dressed people parading around in the lobby.

"Thank you for bringing me to the ballet with you," Nikos said, calling my attention back to him. I looked at his hypnotizing eyes. His allure was unavoidable. I was a prisoner of his charm.

"So… what do you think of the theater?" I asked, smiling shyly at him.

He looked around, appreciating the architecture of the building and the interior decoration. "It's a beautiful, modern theater. I love the contemporary decoration. Do you come here often?"

"Yes, I try to, but sometimes I don't find company."

"What about a… boyfriend?" I took another sip of the wine, wondering if he was going to take the question back as he had done before when he asked me about my perfume. But this time he was waiting for an answer.

"We… we broke up a few months ago. He didn't appreciate the ballet, though," I said, trying to sound casual. Nikos smiled. I didn't want to talk about my personal life with him. "So, what have you been doing on the weekends?" I changed subjects.

"I love going to the museum even on the weekends to see how the public is embracing the exhibit. I'll have more flexibility this week, though, when I rent a car. Being driven around by museum docents is nice, but I want to explore the city on my own," he said. Being driven by museum docents? What about Maggie? He really never talked about her or mentioned her in any capacity. Maybe he was referring to her as one of the museum docents, so no one would realize they were going out? Did his issue about not wanting to socialize with his students

45

and colleagues include his relationship with Maggie? But Maggie behaved like she wasn't hiding or being discreet about their relationship at all. I wanted so much to ask him what was going on between them, but I was afraid the intrusion in his personal life would destroy the mood of the evening. It was better not to. I finished the wine right when we heard the first chime ring, advising patrons to start looking for their seats. We found our seats and waited for the show to start.

It was a magnificent performance and the audience offered a resounding ovation to the dancers at the end of the final act. As we got up to leave, Nikos stepped in front of me and offered me his hand to help me walk down the steep stairs of the theater. His touch was electrifying and I didn't want to let go, but he released my hand as soon as we got down to the foyer.

"Did you enjoy the show?" I asked.

"Very much so. Thank you again for a lovely evening," he answered. "I'd love to take you out for a drink, but I have business to attend to."

"Business? But it's 11:30 pm and it's Saturday…" The words came out of my mouth unexpectedly, as if I doubted him. I should shut up. He was probably going to see Maggie.

"I know it sounds strange, but Athens is eight hours ahead and I need to talk to my museum's associates. We're facing some financial difficulties, and yesterday there was a meeting with a possible benefactor and some investors. Some of our galleries are not even opened due to lack of funds. I don't know yet the results of the meeting, but I need to catch up with them before Monday morning. I may have to shorten my stay here if my presence is required there sooner," Nikos explained. I remembered reading that the National Archaeological Museum was facing financial and public relations troubles partly due to Greece's economic crisis.

"I'm so sorry to hear that. I hope a good solution is on the way," I said. He wasn't going to see Maggie after all, but then, what if he was lying about it?

"Thank you for your concern. I hope so too. I've invested a lot of my time in that museum and I want to make sure it continues to be regarded as a world renowned institution. But I'm very worried about its future." He really sounded preoccupied. We walked to the car and I drove back to his place. He explained to me some of his concerns about the museum's financial situation, and how he hoped he would be able to resolve the issues, so he wouldn't have to return sooner. He was enjoying his stay in Houston, and he was also dealing with the directors of both Chicago and Atlanta's fine art museums, as they were interested in hosting the exhibit. There was a lot on his plate, including heavy negotiations to loan some of the artifacts, which could be very profitable.

I parked next to the gate when we got to his apartment complex.

"I'm sorry I bothered you with my work problems," he said. "I enjoyed the evening and I can't thank you enough. I really needed this break: an enchanting performance of the *Swan Lake*, with lovely company. And *Chance*." He lifted my hand to his lips, brushing my skin lightly with a swift kiss. The feeling of his soft lips on me set my skin on fire. I longed to be held, kissed and loved by this man. How could I resist him? I was his, completely, wholeheartedly, and my soul would hurt forever because I didn't think he would ever be mine.

"It was… a…wonderful evening indeed," I mumbled.

Nikos released my hand and opened the car door. He stepped out, looked back at me, wished me a good night and told me to drive carefully. In an instant, he was gone, like a vanishing mirage. It took me a few minutes to turn on the car again before driving home, inebriated with the feeling of Nikos' lips on my skin. And the pleasure of realizing he had noticed my perfume again.

****

The insistent ring of the phone woke me up. "What are you doing today, girlfriend? Do you want to go to the beach?" Jane asked as soon as I said hello, and I could sense her excitement.

47

I looked at the clock by my bedside table. 8:30 am - on Sunday morning.

"No," I answered shortly. "You know I hate waking up early on Sundays," I said in a bad mood.

"Sorry. I didn't hear from you this weekend, so I thought we might catch up by having some fun in the sun," she said.

"I need to do some work on my research paper. I haven't touched it since I had my session with Nikos."

"Any news about the Greek stud? Have you seen him lately?"

"No." I lied.

"OK, then. Have fun studying. If you change your mind within the next hour give me a call back. And sorry for waking you up, I hope I haven't ruined your morning." she said, cheerfully.

"You haven't. Enjoy the beach. I'll catch up with you tomorrow at the museum. Oh. Can I ask you for a huge favor?" I asked, just remembering I had to take my car in for service on Monday, which would take all day. I needed a ride from the repair shop to the museum in the morning, and back to the shop in the afternoon.

"Sure, I'll pick you up at the repair shop and I'll take you back there after work," Jane said. "And we will do lunch."

"You're the best," I said. I considered going back to bed, but of course, once I was awake, my thoughts were dominated by Nikos. I wondered if he had talked to his associates in Athens and what was the outcome of their meeting with their prospective investors and benefactors. I couldn't imagine him having to go back to Greece sooner than planned. It was going to happen anyhow, but later was better than sooner. My irresistible attraction to him was growing stronger every day. I felt a mutual rising sexual tension between us. The way he looked at me was intimidating, and I'm sure he knew the effect he had on me when I was in his presence. But Maggie's threats telling me to back off were in the back of my mind, reminding me constantly there was something not quite clear about their connection. I really wanted to find out what was going on before I got myself involved with him deeper, if there was any hope at all.

I spent the rest of the day researching and writing my paper on the Greek bronze vases. The notes I took when I was with Nikos were very helpful, but I found myself lacking in material to complete the chapter about the pyxis and I knew I would have to ask for his help again. I thought about giving him a call, but decided against it. I didn't want to push it. It would be better to talk to him directly on Monday, and I would find a way to do so. I was already looking forward to it.

Chapter 8

Monday didn't start very well. As soon as I left home, I noticed I had forgotten the research folder at my desk, so I ran back to the apartment to retrieve it. I wanted to make sure I had it with me when I talked to Nikos sometime during the day. By the time I got to the repair shop, Jane was already there waiting. The manager took the apartment key out of my key chain and handed it to me. I jumped into Jane's car, since we were now running a little late. When we arrived at the museum, I realized I had left my purse in the car but I still had the apartment key, my cell phone, and my research folder, though. I called the repair shop's manager, he found my purse right away, and locked it up in his office, so it was secure until I returned to get the car. Afraid of misplacing the loose apartment key, I inserted it in one of the pockets inside my research folder.

My department was backed up and we had lots of work to do. The redesigning project was running a little behind. We had run into a problem with lack of space for a few of the pieces that needed to be displayed, and the architect was doing some last minute adjustments on the gallery set up. I tried to look for Nikos but had no time to walk to the Antiquities department. During lunch, I decided to give him a call.

"Hi, Nikos, it's Sabrina. I'm sorry to bother you at work," I said when I heard him say hello.

"Hi, Sabrina. You don't bother me. What can I do for you?" He sounded worried.

"Well, I hate to ask you this, but I was working on my paper yesterday and I still need your help. Only if you can spare a few minutes, of course. I know you're busy and there's a lot going on." I almost regretted having called him.

"Of course I'll help you. But I don't have any free time to spend with you during the day today. Do you have your paper with you?"

"Yes, I have it."

"Bring it to me if you don't mind. I'll take a look at it, and we can talk later tonight or we can try to set up something after work

during this week to discuss it. Would that work for you?"

"Sure. You really don't need to do it if you don't have time. I understand you're overwhelmed."

"Sabrina, just bring me your paper. I will work with you," he said in a persuasive voice before hanging up.

"What is going on?" Jane chimed in.

"I need Nikos' help with the paper again. I decided to branch into another type of vessel and now I don't have enough material to finish the chapter. He knows everything about it, as you can imagine."

"How convenient," she teased.

"Jane. I'm serious. I didn't do that on purpose. But if you really want to know... yes, I'm happy I have to ask for his help if it will give me another chance to spend time with him."

"And then? Are you quenching your thirst for the Greek stud?"

"No. I'm helplessly in love with this guy. But I don't know what's going on between him and Maggie."

"Forget about Maggie. Go for it."

"She confronted me last week, Jane. I don't want crazy Maggie to make a scene here, but I told her that if I needed his help, I was going to ask for it. And she would have to deal with it."

"Really? How come you didn't tell me that! Maggie's a crazy bitch, but don't let yourself be intimidated by her. If Nikos is not backing off from helping you, then go for it."

"You're right. I'll bring my research folder to Nikos, and that's it."

As soon as we were done having lunch, I walked to the Antiquities department where Dr. Jones had assigned Nikos a temporary office for the duration of his stay. The door was open, and Nikos was inside, talking in Greek over the phone. He sounded upset and I wondered if the dealings with the investors were not going as planned. I stood by the door, not wanting to interrupt his phone conversation. He turned around and upon seeing me, he bowed, acknowledging my presence, but continued to talk. After a few minutes, he hung up.

"I'm sorry. It was an important call," he said, frowning, as he brought both his hands up to his head sliding his fingers through his hair, and sighed.

"Problems?" I asked, thinking how I would love to soothe him.

"Yeah, something I hope will get resolved soon. Family issues... So, what can I do for you?" He changed subjects quickly, obviously avoiding talking about what was bothering him.

"The pyxis," I said. "I did some research but I can't seem to find enough information to finish the chapter. I brought what I've written so far, if you can take a look..." I handed him my folder. He opened it and briefly looked over the papers.

"Looks like you're doing a great job. There seems to be a lot of good material here."

"I hope so. I really hate to bother you with it knowing you're so busy... if you don't have time, I completely understand. I don't want to be a nuisance."

"You don't bother me at all, Sabrina. I'm looking forward to helping you with this." Nikos stared at me and gave me his sexy faint smile.

"I have to go back to work. I really appreciate all you're doing. I don't even know how to thank you."

"You don't need to thank me. It's my pleasure. I'll get back to you." It was clear Nikos had a lot on his plate and something back in Greece was definitely bothering him. I had assumed it was about the museum, but this time he had mentioned family.

By 5 pm, Jane came looking for me to give me a ride back to the repair shop, which I had totally forgotten about. I briefed her about my quick meeting with Nikos, and how busy he was, but I didn't mention anything about his problems. My ballet date with Nikos was still a secret and I was determined to keep it that way, at least until he was out of the country.

My car was ready, and the manager gave me my purse back. I was relieved everything was working out. But when I got home and tried to open the door, I realized the apartment key was not on the key chain. Oh, no! I remembered taking the apartment key with me and placing it inside the pocket on my research folder, which was now with Nikos. Great. How was I going to enter my home? I didn't want to call him right away. It would be too embarrassing to ask him to come open the door for me, or go to his place to get my keys. I decided the best thing to do for now was to call the locksmith, and get my key from Nikos the next day.

It didn't take long for the locksmith to come and open the door. But I had to make sure to let Nikos know he needed to bring my folder to the museum, in case he had taken it home, so I could have my key back.

"Nikos, it's me, Sabrina."

"Hi. How are you, is everything OK?"

"Yes, well, er… I'm sorry to bother you, but do you have my folder with you, or did you leave it at the museum?"

"I have it with me, but I just got home. I haven't looked at it yet. I rented a car today after I left the museum, and I got home later than usual," he said.

"I didn't mean to rush you, it's not that. It's… this is really embarrassing… I accidentally left my apartment key inside the folder and I wanted to make sure you brought it to the museum tomorrow."

"You left your apartment key inside your research folder?" he asked, confused. I told him what had happened at the car repair shop, and how I forgot and misplaced my purse and keys. I heard him laugh. "You're lucky you got your purse back and didn't lose your key," he said, amused by my ordeal. "You should have called me before getting the locksmith. I would have brought you the key."

"Thank you, I've been bothering you enough already. I can get the key tomorrow."

"Are you sure you don't need it today? I can bring you the key and your research paper later tonight when I'm done reading it.

I'm going to print some material I have from an archaeological publication, this way you will have some more reading to do before finishing your chapter."

"That's fantastic! I'd love that. You really don't need to rush and come over to give me the key back today. You're probably busy and…" He didn't let me finish.

"I'll make time for you. Just text me your address and I will come over a little later to return your key and paper, if you'd like."

"Yes, sure, I'd like that," I mumbled.

He hung up and I texted him my address. I couldn't believe Nikos was coming over to my apartment, and I had no idea how soon he would arrive. Why didn't I ask? It could be in 10 minutes or two hours. I needed to relax. I poured myself a glass of white wine and prepared a hot, bubbly bath. I was sure I'd have enough time to relax before he came knocking at my door.

Chapter 9

Nikos didn't knock. He used the key to open the door and walked in unceremoniously, looking for me. The door to the bathroom was ajar and he walked in slowly, with no constraint, finding me submersed in the bathtub. He took me completely by surprise, and I let out a gasp as soon as I saw him by the door. I wasn't expecting him to come over that soon, and much less to just walk in while I was taking a bath. I stared at him in sheer shock as he started undressing slowly, and I kept watching him from my cover of bubbles and perfumed foam.

He unbuttoned his shirt, one button at a time, slowly, almost rhythmically, and his eyes were on me the whole time while he revealed his toned chest. I was speechless. I thought I was dreaming. He took his shoes off and moved on to unzip his jeans. They fell on the floor over his shirt. Gradually, without taking his eyes off me, Nikos pulled off the last piece of clothing covering his masculine tanned body, exhibiting a statuesque wonder I had seen only in art books and in my imagination when I had fantasized about him. He slipped carefully into the bathtub behind me, without asking my permission, because he already knew I could not stop him. He held the soapy sponge and started rubbing my back; moving in circles and making the tension vanish. Then, he placed his strong arms around me until his hands cupped my breasts, massaging them while kissing my neck and shoulders. He felt my nipples getting hard and squeezed them between his fingers, sending chills down my spine and all through me. His wet and curious hands kept moving around them, caressing, feeling my perfect round breasts which fit so well into his possessive hands.

Hot water and foam added to the thrill and excitement. He kissed my neck and head, sliding his hands over my chest, traveling down to my navel and delving into the slippery skin of my body until he reached the deep mound between my legs. I could not help but open them wider to his curious exploration, while moaning and sighing in pleasure. He moved swiftly, making no sound while he aroused the woman in me like no one had ever done before. His fingers were caressing the folds of my most feminine part, opening me and probing me. Sliding in and out, his fingers sensed the strength of my inner muscles and felt my dripping juice mingle with the hot and soapy water of the tub.

Instead of allowing me to reach my ecstasy, he pulled his fingers away from me, and before I could protest the interruption of such sensual feeling, he grabbed my own hands and guided them towards his magnificent hardness. Like a perfect statue from the mythology books and ancient Greek art I had in my library, his hard and muscled body was ready to penetrate mine and take over my burning passion. The tension that had been building since we met a few days ago was now getting to its peak. There was no denying a mutual sexual intensity had been brewing between us. It was real. No longer a dream that made me fantasize about his masculine and chiseled body taking me, having me, giving way to my desires and making me a woman.

I turned around and mounted him. He slid inside of me easily and perfectly. I was moaning with pleasure, feeling the thrusting of his body inside of me complete my own movements. I danced on top of him, riding the Greek god of my dreams, holding on to him while his hands pressed on my waist, moving me back and forth to his pulsating rhythm. I moved my face closer to his, opening my mouth to receive his wet tongue. Kissing passionately, our tongues explored, moving slower; our lips brushed against each other, licking and tasting. His mouth moved down, kissing my chin, neck and chest until he found my hard nipples again, and at once nibbled at one, increasing the pressure of his lips to suck, lick, and bite, alternating between both of them.

His tongue moved around while his lips and teeth teased my nipples, and I could feel him growing harder and deeper inside of me. We both felt the climax arriving in this inconceivable

56

dance of bodies, and as he was releasing his orgasm, he heard me scream with pleasurable delight. I could still feel the thrusting while the hot and wet semen flooded inside of me, mixing up with my own juices and fulfilling my longing and passion for Nikos. We let ourselves float with abandon in the steamy water of the tub, caressing and kissing gently, waiting for our hearts to resume their normal beating after this ecstatic experience. He held me tight in his arms, in silence, and I did not want him to let me go. Ever. I did not want this to be over, I wanted to keep kissing him and making love to him until we were both exhausted and could no longer move. I dared not say a word, so afraid I was to spoil this perfect and passionate moment. A moment I had dreamed of so much.

We got out of the tub, wrapping each other in my soft cotton towels, tapping and drying slowly, while we continued kissing. Then, he suddenly picked me up and carried me straight to bed, both of us still naked and barely dried from the erotic bath. He placed me gently on the bed, and for the first time he took a long look at my exposed body. I trembled in reaction to his look. He somehow frightened me with his eyes showing so much desire. I could feel the heat emanating from his dark skinned body and was not surprised when I realized he was again ready to intrude me.

Stroking my wet long brown hair with the back of his hand, his eyes still admiring and observing every response of my body from his touches, he kissed me again. His luscious lips, now fuller with the lust growing inside once more, touched mine, and he parted my lips with his tongue, invading my mouth in pleasurable abandon. His kisses grew stronger, firmer, and then slowed down again, lips just barely brushing against each other and then opening wide once more to swallow mouth and tongue in an aroused and passionate dance. I could not resist him. I knew I was his.

His mouth continued its investigation of my body. While his hands caressed every inch of my silky skin, his lips moved down my breasts, teasing my nipples again, kissing, sucking,

57

nibbling, and biting, making my body swerve in anguish under him. Like in my dream, I was a nymph spreading my legs to expose my dripping private opening, and as soon as the Greek god realized the movements of my hips going back and forth, begging for the release of my growing anxiety, he plunged his mouth inside of me, making me moan in utter torment.

Holding my legs up with both his strong hands, Nikos revealed even more of me to the discovery of his hungry mouth. His tongue kept going in and out, caressing me with kisses and long licks, reaching for my most sensitive skin, flicking and teasing me. My hips moved in a frenzied way, back and forth, ready to receive his invasion once again. His hands moved to my buttocks, grabbing and pressing them hard, lifting them to accommodate his mouth and insatiable tongue inside of me, making me wriggle wildly. I clutched the sides of the bed, holding on to the sheets until I could no longer resist the increasing tension, and exploded in a sensational orgasm, screaming and crying, unable to hold on to such powerful feeling.

Nikos moved away from me just enough to look at my weakened and satiated body, wasted in bed, completely abandoned to his mercy. But I knew it was not over. Glancing at him, I could see, more than before, how ready he was to take me again. Without resistance, I offered myself once more to him. He slid inside of me without hesitation. I was shuddering with delight, having him again going in and out while I was slippery with my own juices, and I wanted him to make me his forever.

He grabbed my legs and lifted them straight up, thrusting back and forth, shoving deep and low, not allowing me to rest. He rendered me a prisoner of his insatiable appetite and virile urge to possess me. How long could I last? The indescribable excitement was beyond words, felt only when there was such perfect union of bodies, a total completion of passion. A desire so irresistible that defied the barriers of my understanding, so lustful and powerful, throwing us, two human beings, in complete and savage impetuosity to the indulgence of flesh and body, with unappeasable longing and carnality. I had been waiting for this since I fell in love with him at first sight. This evening was beyond my expectations. I could never think the Greek god I had been longing for was so much more than I could imagine. It was a night I would treasure forever, for as long as I lived. This intimate moment made me more of a woman than I had ever been my entire life.

With the excitement of our passionate love making, he reached his climax again, exploding inside of me with an ardent desire. Our bodies rested. Lying down next to me, he caressed my face and hair, looking me in the eyes and waiting for me to react to his love. I turned around to hug him and held him tight in my arms, resting my head on his shoulder, snuggling together as if we were one and would never be apart. I could not even conceive of him not being there with me. I felt we were the only people in the universe, and all that mattered to me was to never be away from Nikos. I wanted to love him more, to take care of him, to be with him and please him forever. But those feelings frightened me. This physical desire, this fiery chemistry between us might be the only thing bringing us together in the first place. Or it could be the only thing to tear us apart forever. And that was my biggest fear. Then, there was Maggie. I didn't want to think about it. I wanted to enjoy this moment as much as I could.

I didn't want to disturb the perfect harmony of our bodies together by getting into conversation and I wasn't sure he wanted me to express myself. Instead of words, I kept pressing my body against his, feeling the soft texture of his lush bronzed skin, almost like a statue made of silky smooth chocolate, yet as hard as marble. His masculine body was just as I had always visualized it in my dreams: picture perfect, taken from the mold of a real Greek god or hero, Narcissus, Adonis, Hercules, or Zeus himself. Nikos was my dream and I was completely captivated by his charm. I would surrender to him forever. I closed my eyes, immersed in an embrace with him, not letting go, feeling his body, his breath, his delicious fragrance, and his heartbeats next to mine. His hands touched my hair. I was in a dream. And a dream it was, for when I woke up a little later, he was no longer in my bed.

I looked around for him in the apartment. It was 3 am. No traces of his presence were even there for me to feel. Had I dreamed again? No, it was not possible - it had been too real. I found the key he used to come in on top of the table by my bed, along with my research folder. There were comments scribbled inside, as well as print-outs of archaeological journals talking about pyxis. Yes, I remember he mentioned he was going to print something for me to read. I did not know what to think of it. I blamed myself for not talking to him, for falling asleep, for not waking up when he moved away from me. How could I have let him go? How could he leave me without a word? I went around looking for a note, or anything that might tell me he had really been there, that I was not dreaming, that he would come back. My search was in vain. There were no sign he had even been there, except for the key and folder on the table, and his scent on my bed, which I knew was real. Nikos had been in my bed. But what was I going to do? How would I even look at his face when I saw him in the museum again? What was I thinking when I let him get into my place like that and make love to me so passionately without resisting? I went back to bed and buried myself in the sheets, longing to be with him again, longing for his body, for his kisses, for Nikos.

Chapter 10

It had been an agonizing few days for me after what happened between us. I couldn't believe I hadn't seen Nikos, or heard from him. Every day I came to the museum hoping to see him, but I didn't have courage to walk to his department and look for him. Why hadn't he called me? With a heavy pain in my heart, I was forced to realize our night together must have meant nothing to him. But I remembered all the intimate moments, and vividly recounted all the gestures and touches from that unforgettable evening. It was excruciating to think about it. I had been really busy with work and it had helped me endure the days without any news from him, but the knowledge we were both working under the same roof was earth shattering. I felt so empty, so hurt, and at the same time, so stupid for having allowed myself to be in this situation.

And seeing him standing there, in front of me all of a sudden was pure torture. I didn't know what to do. Nikos looked so distant. With his wavy black hair mussed up and carelessly combed, his penetrating dark eyes glanced at me nonchalantly, and his body movements were not giving away any detectable emotion, making me wonder what he might be thinking. Still, he looked irresistible wearing a pair of jeans and a white button down shirt with the sleeves rolled up. I was speechless, motionless, caught off guard by the surprise of this unplanned encounter just outside the museum's main entrance.

He was there, right in front of me, and to my disappointment, he did not seem excited to see me. I gathered enough courage to say hi. He bowed his head, almost as if avoiding eye contact with me, and I walked away quickly towards the museum's gift shop, shaking. I was absolutely disconcerted. I had to talk to him, to know what was going on, to kiss him, to hold him, to love him again. I craved his touch, his mouth, his body. I could not stand this torment any longer but I was too uncomfortable to face him.

To my surprise, he turned around and walked after me to the gift shop. I had to say something. I had to at least say goodbye, if that's what it was coming to. I could not bear to see him and pretend it had just been a dream, but I had no courage to do anything. He moved towards me slowly while I glanced through an art catalog. I felt his presence in front of me and immediately felt chills running through my veins. My body was already aching for him. I trembled in anticipation, knowing too well my voice would falter if I decided to say something. Nikos glimpsed at me casually, waiting for me to finish browsing the catalog.

"Hi, Nikos. Would you like to join me for coffee?" That was all I could mutter while he stood there watching me.

"Of course," he said with that husky and sexy voice. Courteously, he led me to the door and we entered the museum's coffee shop. He ordered two espressos and we sat at a corner table facing each other. I sensed the tension. His facial muscles were tight, his high brows curved, making his eyes bigger and his long lashes gave them a somber and mysterious look.

"I owe you an apology," he started.

"An apology?" I asked, surprised.

"I'm sorry", he said. "I've been really busy. I know it's my fault. I am terribly sorry for what happened."

I had a horrible feeling the ardent evening we spent together was a one night stand when I never heard back from him. Nothing more than hot sex, or good memories he would take back home. Maybe it was time for me to tell him what I felt and how overwhelmed I was with everything that happened between us physically. But if he was apologizing for what happened, it could only mean he regretted it.

"You… you're sorry for what happened?" I could barely speak.

"Sabrina," he said, "I'm very sorry for what I did to you. I invaded your privacy, I violated your intimacy. I feel like I raped you, and you have all the right to be upset and confused. I could not expect you to call me after I broke into your house. What was I thinking? After what I did to you that evening, all I beg is for you to forgive me, please. I apologize. I did not mean to insult you or offend you in any way. I have no right to provoke you and I feel miserable knowing I may have caused you pain."

I looked at Nikos in astonishment. How could he think he had violated me or offended me by making love to me so passionately? I stared at him speechless before I gathered courage to talk.

"Nikos, no, it is not that. You didn't do anything against my will. Not at all. This is not how I feel, this is all wrong. No, it's not your fault, it's mine. You don't need to apologize."

His piercing and intimidating dark eyes invaded me, looking deep into my soul and making me feel naked and bare and completely subjected to his power. I could feel the uncomfortable wetness in between my legs. I knew it was going to be hard to conceal my desire. I was exposed and he knew it. I knew he could smell the sexual instinct in me and he could provoke me if he wanted to.

"Why is it your fault? Tell me, then, what you want me to do, because I don't want to hurt you." I stared into his eyes. He had me completely under his spell. What did I want him to do after an evening that was imprinted in my memory forever? A memory... a memory like a cloud that has a distinct shape and a minute later vanishes just like smoke in the sky, with no definition, no clarity, no consistency and no meaning. Why was he apologizing? Why did he think it was his fault? I knew he was busy and had a lot on his plate. I was a fool. I had to tell him what I wanted him to do. I needed him. I wanted him more than anything I ever wanted in my life. And I didn't care if I sounded crazy, or out of my mind. I longed for his touch, for his love, for him to take me again. I didn't want that night to be over. I wanted more, not a one night stand. I took a sip of the espresso getting colder on the table, and looked at him. While I thought about an answer, I went back in time and re-lived the wonderful moments I had spent with him just a few days ago. I didn't know whether to tell him I missed him so much, or if I should just forget about it. Should I admit I was afraid to hear him say he didn't care for me and what happened between us that evening was nothing of importance to him?

Before I had time to answer his question, Maggie walked hastily into the coffee shop, obviously looking for him. She approached our table without excusing herself for the interruption, and reminded Nikos of an appointment he had with Dr. Jones, who was

already waiting in his office. She barely looked at me.

"I'm sorry, Sabrina, I'm very sorry, but I have to go," and before I could say anything else, Maggie rushed him out the door, looking back at me in a threatening way. I finished my espresso and walked out of the museum as soon as I could, with tears streaming down my face. At the parking lot, I sat silently in my car, waiting for the tears to dry so I could drive far away from this museum that only reminded me of Nikos. But my refuge was no better than the museum, for the place I lived was the only testimony to all the wonderful hours I spent in his arms, making love to him, being his and feeling like the woman I thought I would never be again. I was making a fool of myself. I should never have allowed Nikos to walk into my place and make love with me, knowing he was dating Maggie. What was I thinking?

I called my department's curator and told her I was not feeling well, and would not work today. There was no way I could go back to the museum and work as if I hadn't seen Nikos at all. And Maggie. I felt awful. What had happened between us? Why did he think he violated me? Was he feeling guilty because he betrayed Maggie by making love to me? Shocked and confused, I drove home.

I wasn't surprised when Jane came furiously knocking at the door later in the afternoon. After all, I had avoided her most of the week and I didn't show up for work. She could tell I had been crying. Coldplay's *True Love* was streaming on Pandora. Listening to the lyrics made me feel so sad. Chris Martin was singing about lost love and imploring his loved one to tell him one more time that she loved him, even if it was a lie. Oh, Nikos, you can lie to me and love me just one more time.

"What happened to you? Why are you listening to this sad song? Are you love sick?" Jane asked.

"No... I don't know... Yes, of course, I am..."

Chris Martin's voice continued on the speakers, asking the object of his love to lie to him, and even calling it true love. How pathetic I felt. The song didn't help.

"You've been crying? What is going on? Did Maggie attack you or something?"

"It's a long story. I haven't told anyone about it." The song kept playing.

"I have all evening, my dear. Open up, but turn that begging song off," Jane said.

I had to vent. I really had to tell her what was going on, for my own sanity. I stopped the music. I just couldn't keep these feelings inside of me any longer. I needed to sort things out and I needed a friend. So I spilled the story out to Jane. She listened to me intently, not once interrupting my narration. I ended up telling her about going to the ballet with Nikos, about his policy of not going out with students and colleagues, about how he kissed my hand, the growing sexual innuendo between us, and his showing up at my apartment a few days ago culminating with the most stupendous love making I had ever had in my life. And of course, our brief and painful encounter earlier today. When I finished, I had tears in my eyes again. It hurt to think about Nikos.

"I don't know what to tell you," Jane said. "I can't believe he just had the guts to walk into your place and have the most incredible sex with you and you guys didn't even say a word to each other. That's surreal. And you actually don't even know him."

"I was dreaming. He is a god," I mumbled. "What am I going to do?"

"One thing is certain, you can't avoid him. You can't stop going to the museum and jeopardize the completion of your internship. You have to be strong. And you have to stop drowning in self-pity. Listening to sad songs imploring for love won't help you."

65

"I know. One part of me wished Nikos would go back to Greece sooner. The other part desperately wants him here. But I need to talk to him. I need to let him know it's not his fault. I allowed him to, I didn't stop him. I wanted him to continue. Regardless of the outcome, I have to tell him how I feel."

Jane shook her head in agreement. "What if he tells you it was a mistake and he shouldn't have done it? Are you prepared to hear that?"

"Of course not. But I have to - I don't know what to expect. I have no idea what is going on in his mind, about me, Maggie, the issues he's facing with his museum back in Greece... and something about his family," I said. I had to be strong. It was possible Nikos would totally reject me.

"I hate to tell you this, but maybe he needed to escape that evening because he was too overwhelmed... and you were the perfect break for him. I mean, think about it... there's Maggie keeping him on a leash, financial issues with his museum, family problems, the prospect of going back sooner... The guy needed a break. And you were the perfect victim."

"I hope that was not the case... You haven't heard anything else about his relationship with Maggie, have you?" I asked.

"You know Curt is working with him, right? Every once in a while he mentions how Maggie is always coming around, like a stalker. She doesn't leave Nikos alone. She's always checking who is working with him and making sure he is following his schedule. She seems to be suffocating him."

"But what is his reaction? He's letting her, isn't he?"

"I don't know. Robert thinks she's one of the volunteer docents the museum appointed to serve as his sort of guide or secretary, but Curt keeps convincing him Maggie's having an affair with Nikos."

"A guide or secretary?" I asked, a hint of hope coming back to me, ignoring the last part of her sentence.

"I don't think it makes sense, if you think about it. She's way all over him to be his guide. Has he ever said anything about Maggie to you?"

"Not to me, no, of course not. He wouldn't, if he had intentions of going to bed with me," I stated, saddened by the thought.

"Right, but as far as we know, he told you he doesn't go out with students or colleagues, and you were an exception. But he was with Maggie when we met them at Theo's. Robert's reasoning is that he was being driven around by a docent before he rented a car – and that's what Maggie pretty much told me when we met them at Theo's – she was driving him around. They're really keeping it as a huge secret, and he's a good actor, because she certainly isn't."

"I don't know, Jane. This is all too confusing. Maggie confronted me and told me to back off from talking to her *boyfriend*. I should not have let Nikos make love to me without knowing what the situation was."

"You will just have to find out. I suggest you start by asking him directly what his involvement with Maggie is. And go from there," Jane said.

I felt better. Talking to Jane about the whole situation relieved part of my tension and made me feel somewhat cheerful. Avoiding Nikos and not going to the museum were childish actions, and I had to get over it. I had one night with the guy and I was already feeling that miserable. The best course of action was to have a hearty conversation with Nikos and expose my fears and doubts about what had happened between us, and find out if there would be any kind of future whatsoever.

After Jane left, I decided to face my reality and went back to work on my research paper. Since the evening Nikos had walked into my apartment and left the folder there, I had not touched it. I opened it and read his remarks. It looked like he had graded a paper, making comments on the sides and throwing in suggestions for improvement. I let out a smile. He was great with his job and he had really given time and attention to my research. How could I not love him? I was absorbed in the reading material he had printed out for me, when my cell rang. Thinking it was Jane, I picked it up without noticing the caller ID. I answered the phone happily. "Are you checking on me already?" I said. There was no reply. "Hello?"

"Sabrina?" My heart skipped a beat. The unmistakable husky voice was calling my name.

"H-Hello, Nikos. I'm sorry, I thought it was Jane," I said, almost choking.

"Are you OK? I heard you didn't work today."

"Yes, I'm fine. Thanks for your concern. I'll be back tomorrow," I managed to say. My voice was barely audible. I wasn't expecting his call.

"I'd like to talk to you. In person. I really owe you a big apology and I'm very sorry for my behavior towards you. If you're not busy tomorrow afternoon, could you come see me at my office after five? I have a few lectures to prepare and will be there later." Oh my. Going to see him tomorrow in his office to hear what he had to say. An apology. Nikos, I don't want your apology, I want you. I want you to tell me you love me and if you don't, then lie, lie to me. The sad song was still on my mind.

"No, I don't have any plans. I can come over to your office after five then."

"Thank you. I'll see you tomorrow." He hung up. I read a couple more pages of the material he had brought over to me and tried to write another paragraph, but I couldn't put any words on paper. There was only one thing on my mind, and it was Nikos. And I kept replaying his voice inviting me to come to his office tomorrow after work. How would all of this end if it had barely started? I went to bed, hoping my Greek god would come visit his nymph again at least in erotic dreams.

Chapter 11

I decided not to tell Jane about my upcoming meeting with Nikos or his phone call the night before. I was too anxious about it, and it was better if I didn't have her cheering me on or making me more worried about what might happen. I'd prefer to tell her about it later. I'm glad the day went by real fast. I had so much to catch up with from being absent the day before, which didn't allow me idle time to be daydreaming about Nikos. At 5 pm, I put my working tools away, left the department with my other colleagues, and walked into the restroom to make sure I looked presentable before I met Nikos. OK, I thought to myself, you look fine. It would be better if I didn't tease him, so I decided not to refresh my perfume. I just dabbed some lip gloss on my lips to give me a fresher look.

The door to Nikos' temporary office was closed. I approached it carefully, trying to find out if I could hear him inside. I heard his voice speaking in Greek but I didn't want to interrupt him. He sounded upset, his voice at times rising almost as if he was yelling, then suddenly it would go down to almost a whisper, as if he was issuing a threat. It was hard to tell. I wished I had studied Modern Greek. I waited a few minutes until there was only silence, then, I knocked lightly. The voice that echoed from the other side of the door was quick and almost angry. "Come in."

I entered the room unhurriedly, afraid I was interrupting him. He sat by the computer typing something in Greek and looked up as soon as he heard the door open. His expression softened when he saw me and he gave me his faint smile.

"Hi," Nikos said. "Thank you for coming, please have a seat and close the door." I did as he asked, while he turned his back to me to continue typing. "Just a minute, please," he said. I waited for him to finish his task. Being in the same room with him brought back all the memories of his lovemaking and instinctively, my nipples got harder and I felt moisture. Nikos finished typing and turned to face me.

"How are you doing?" he asked.

I cleared my throat, knowing my voice would falter. "Doing better. Thanks."

Nikos stared at me trying to read my facial expression, but his phone rang, and he let out a loud sigh before answering it. While he talked in Greek again, he looked at me shaking his head and lifted his finger, motioning for me to wait. The office he was using was a large one with a huge window facing the tree lined street down below. It was a nice view. I got up from the chair and walked to the window while I waited for Nikos to end his phone conversation. When he finished talking, he stood up from his chair and came closer to where I stood facing the window. I sensed his body next to me and a chill ran through my spine. I didn't realize he was so close to me when I turned to face him and felt my cheeks start to burn.

"Why are you blushing?" he asked. I knew he could notice every reaction of my body when he was next to me.

"You have no idea what you do to me," I blurted out. It was too much being so close to him. I could smell his sweet scent and I wanted desperately to be in his arms.

"What do I do to you?" he teased, talking in a rasping voice that was almost a whisper, and stepped closer to me, giving me no room to move. He looked at me with his soulful, deep-set brown eyes, and his dark, striking countenance emanated an intensity I'd never felt before. I was shaking, suffocated by his overwhelming presence. I opened my mouth trying to gasp for air, while unexpectedly he pinned me against the wall, lifted my arms over my head and lowered his head to kiss me. I was rendered helpless. I wanted to fight him, to stop his advances, to close my lips from the forceful entry of his sweet tongue now exploring every inch of my mouth. But I had no strength to fight him. I wanted him. I wanted to feel his kisses and his body on me again since that afternoon in my apartment. I opened my mouth to eagerly receive his advances and my body moved in excitement. I lifted my legs, encircling his waist with them, attaching my pelvis to his hips so I could feel him better. I was too aroused by this man who had an unbelievable effect

70

on me. All of a sudden, he released my arms and delicately pulled my legs down from around him. My feet touched the floor again. He stepped back, detaching himself from me. My heart pounded so hard I thought they were drums. He glanced at me and turned around, running his fingers nervously through his hair before sitting down.

"I'm sorry. Please forgive me. I can't do this to you. I have to control myself," he said.

I didn't move. Everything he did astonished me. I had no idea what was going through his mind.

"Forgive you for what? What do you want me to forgive you for? What do you have to control yourself for?" I asked in despair. I wanted him more than anything and I had no idea why he was acting so erratic, what was bothering him, and why he had kissed me and then released me all of a sudden. Why was he rejecting me? Was it Maggie?

"Forgive me for invading your house, your privacy, your body. I shouldn't have done this to you. I don't want to hurt you. I shouldn't have walked into your place like that. I shouldn't have touched you. I'm sorry, I really am."

"I don't want your apology," I muttered, disappointed.

"Why did you come here?" he asked.

"Because you asked me to, didn't you?" I answered, visibly upset and almost choking. He was rejecting me and I was not ready for it.

"No. I mean, yes I asked you to come. But why did you really come? I just offered you an apology, and you don't want it. So what is it that you want from me?" His voice was calm, but his eyes penetrated my soul without compassion. I didn't understand him, but I had to open my heart and tell him what I really felt. What did he really want to know?

"I don't want your apology because… because I want you, Nikos. I came here because I wanted to see you. Because I missed you. Because I can't get you out of my mind. Now you know what I want. Is this what you expected to hear from me? Do you regret what happened between us? Why shouldn't you have touched me?" I sobbed, turning my back to him. I stared out the window while tears flooded my eyes, but I didn't want him to see me crying. I closed my eyes, shaking inside, and a few tears trickled down my cheeks. I heard him getting up from the chair and walking towards me again. I didn't want to turn around and face him. His masculine hands closed in on my waist, enveloping me in a secure embrace, and I felt his heavy breathing on my neck. He kissed me softly behind my ears, and down my neck. I felt tingles of excitement running through my skin and couldn't believe this was happening again. I was in his arms, exactly where I wanted to be. I wanted to be his, but this whirlwind of emotions made me dizzy as if I was riding a roller coaster. Oh, my Olympian god, what were you doing to your mere mortal nymph? He gently turned me around to face him. I kept my eyes closed, but he saw the thin stream of tears that had run down my face and dried the tiny drops with his thumbs.

"Of course I don't regret it, but I don't want to hurt you. I'm sorry. I don't want to see you like this," he said, kissing my face where he had just wiped the tears. I opened my eyes but didn't know what to say or what to do. He was so gentle, so delicate, and so lovable. I didn't want to say anything else to ruin this perfectly tender moment. I longed for him. My whole body ached in anticipation of being taken by him once more. The spell was broken by the buzz of his cell phone. I don't know what was happening, but those calls were clearly upsetting him. He released me and answered the phone but this time, though, he spoke in English.

"I told you I am busy tonight. I can't," he said to the person on the other line. He looked away from me, facing the window. "I will try tomorrow, but I can't promise anything right now. There's too much going on and I have to talk to my associates in Greece before I compromise. I will talk to your father about it as soon as I have an agreement from Greece." He hung up and for a second he didn't move. Then, he walked back slowly towards me, wrapped his arms around my waist and stared intently into my eyes, as if trying to validate what I had said moments before.

"So you really don't want my apology?" he asked. I smelled his masculine scent and felt his sweet breath in my face. His mouth was almost closing in on mine.

I smiled. "No, I don't want your apology. It was my fault. I didn't stop you when you came into my apartment."

"Why didn't you?"

"Because... I couldn't... It has never happened to me before. You caught me completely off guard. I mean... you just walked in..." I faltered, looking at him with desire in my eyes. Just remembering what had happened that evening was enough to make me melt in his arms. I wanted him again and I was sure he could sense it. He lowered his head and his lips delicately touched mine. He nibbled lightly on my lips before I opened my mouth to taste him, and I kissed him passionately. His tongue explored my mouth again, and I wrapped my arms around his strong, square shoulders, bringing him closer to me and noticing how hard he was. His kiss became more intense and fierce. His hands found the edge of my shirt and moved underneath it, going up to my bra and lifting it to find my already erect nipples. I let out a soft moan when his fingers pinched my nipples, and immediately felt the uncomfortable wetness between my legs. His tongue slid out of my mouth and he kissed my neck, moving up to my ear lobe, biting it gently with his lips. I brought one of my hands up to the front of his body and cupped his hardness, feeling his excitement growing as he moved his hands out from under my blouse to pull it over my head and with a quick movement, unfastened my bra and let it fall on the floor, exposing my swollen breasts. Nikos stopped kissing me and looked at me, his eyes resting on my chest.

"You are a beautiful goddess, my Aphrodite. I can't resist you," he whispered. I closed my eyes and sighed, and lifted my hands to touch his hair, lowering his head so my lips could meet his again.

"Dr. Soulis, are you in there?" A loud knock at the door startled us. Someone was calling out for Nikos. He released his grip on my body, picked my shirt up from the floor and gave it back to me so I could cover myself.

"Yes, I'm here working. Is there a problem?" Nikos called back without opening the door, waiting for me to get dressed.

"This is Ramon, the security officer, sir," the man replied.

Nikos combed his fingers through his disheveled hair and motioned for me to scoot over to the side, so the man wouldn't see me right away when he opened the door.

"What can I do for you, Officer Ramon?" he asked when he faced the short, skinny man in uniform in front of his office.

"I'm sorry to interrupt your work, Dr. Soulis, but Miss Wallendorf is at the front entrance looking for you. The museum is closed, so we can't let her in. She said she called you but you didn't answer. What do you want me to do with her?" Ramon asked.

Miss Wallendorf... looking for him? Was he referring to *her* father when he talked on the phone a few minutes ago? I couldn't believe this. I couldn't believe Nikos was kissing me and almost making love to me in his office while his girlfriend, Maggie Wallendorf, was looking for him. I was distraught. Again, it was my own fault. I should have restrained myself from falling into his arms before finding out what the situation between them was, and I had failed myself miserably. I gulped, trying to compose myself so I could walk out of his office with my last hint of dignity.

"If you don't mind, please tell her I'll be there in five minutes. Thank you," Nikos told the man before closing the door behind him. I heard Officer Ramon's steps fading away quickly on the hard marble floor of the gallery. I picked up my purse from the table and moved towards the door in silence. I didn't want to say anything else to him. I was deeply disappointed and heartbroken, but upset at myself for being so naïve. *'I don't want to hurt you'*– his words echoed in my mind. That's why he was so intent on apologizing. Because he knew he was going to hurt me. Because of Maggie.

"Where are you going?" He seemed surprised to see me walking towards the door.

"I think you're late to meet your girlfriend," I said, irritated.

"What are you talking about?"

"Well, Nikos, everyone knows you and Maggie are… dating, or whatever. I'm the only fool who didn't want to believe it, because of what happened between us."

"What do you mean everyone knows Maggie and I are dating? What kind of joke is that?" He sounded upset. I gaped at him. Was he pretending there was nothing between them? Was this a part of his seducing game? Maggie was outside waiting for him. The last thing I wanted was to have a brawl with her, for I'm sure she would not be happy to see me walking out of the closed museum next to Nikos. I didn't want to see her. I wanted to get out of there as soon as possible, and try to forget about him. I opened the door to his office without answering him, but he grabbed my arm before I could step out.

"Stay here and wait for me. I won't be long. We need to talk." But as his cell phone started to buzz again, I took advantage of the momentary distraction to free myself from his grip.

"Let me go. She's waiting for you." I walked away as fast as I could without looking back, and chose the employees' exit on the other side of the building where I was able to leave without running into Maggie.

Chapter 12

There were several voice messages from Jane on my cell phone. I knew if I didn't answer her, she would end up coming over to my place to find out what was going on. It was Saturday, and we hadn't seen each other since the day she came over to find out why I had called in sick. Just a few days ago I was heartbroken, and then I got my hopes high again, just to be disappointed once more the next day. Even though my instincts were telling me to run away from Nikos, my heart still belonged to him. And although my heart denied it, I knew having an amorous relationship with the Greek god was impossible. I kept trying to convince myself I would gain nothing from being involved with Nikos. He was going back to Greece soon, to a land far away where the likelihood of seeing him again was as far as the land itself. I knew better long distance relationships were not meant to last. So I had to admit to myself my brief affair with Nikos had to be considered a summer fling, although every cell of my body yearned for more. The worst part was yet to come, for I had to endure knowing he was in town, working under the same roof for at least another month, and there was nothing I could do to avoid bumping into him or Maggie. I decided to call Jane back and briefly tell her about my latest misadventure with Nikos. I needed to snap out of this curse and stop dreaming of Olympus.

"That's awful, Sabrina. I can't believe this. So bitchy Maggie was after your Greek god while he was messing with you in his office? I'm sorry I told you to go after him. That was not good advice."

"It was my fault, Jane. I have to admit I should have asked him questions about his intentions before I allowed myself to be seduced. I can't resist this man. I don't know what to do to get out of his spell. When I see him I completely melt, he's hypnotic…"

"Yeah, but that's not an excuse for his behavior. If he's going out with Maggie, and for sure there's something going on between them, he had no business kissing you and making out with you in his office. Or invading your place and making love to you in the first place."

"He didn't want me to leave his office. He asked me to wait while he was going to talk to Maggie. But I didn't wait. I left him so he could run to her arms. What could he possibly explain to me after that?"

"I'm glad you left. Nikos sounds like a hypocrite. He tells you he doesn't like to go out with students or colleagues, but he's actually trying to be with both you and Maggie. I hate to give you any advice at this point, but if I were you I would try to forget about him," Jane said.

"You're right. I'll try to stay away from the Antiquities department as much as possible and I will put my research on hold until after Nikos is gone. This is so painful. I never thought I would fall head over heels in love so fast and so brutally… Nikos was all I ever dreamed of, and now my dream is shattered, with broken pieces all over the place. It will be next to impossible for me to find someone like him again… and the memories of his touch, his body…"

"Stop, Sabrina," Jane interrupted me. "You'll find someone else. You're young and beautiful and intelligent and Nikos is not the only man in the world."

"Nikos is the only man for me…" I said with tears in my eyes. I still couldn't believe I was so in love with this man, even though I knew almost nothing about him and his life, except for his education.

"The party at Curt and Robert's is tonight, and I'm coming to pick you up. I don't want to hear any excuses. You *are* coming," Jane said before hanging up. I had forgotten all about their get together and was not planning on going. After all, I was not in the mood to socialize, but I knew Jane wouldn't leave me wallowing by myself.

By 6:30 pm, Jane was downstairs waiting for me. I wore a floral print sun dress and high heeled sandals, and let my long brown hair fall loosely over my bare shoulders. Nikos' kisses were still too vivid on my mind and I knew I was going to have a hard time being in a festive gathering with people who only reminded me of him. Not a perfect place to try to forget about him, but at least I was going to be among friends.

Curt and Robert were delighted to see us. They loved to entertain people in their house and threw theme parties almost every month. I was not surprised to realize the party theme was Greece. As long as the Greek Bronze Vessels exhibit was showing in the museum, everything Greek would be *in* for the Art History students participating in the internship. Several of our classmates were already there, including two of the museum's curators with whom Curt had been working in the Antiquities department. The place was decorated with Greek flags, pictures of Greek mythological creatures and archaeological objects, including a fake bronze vase and a statue of Hades, which appropriately reminded me I was in love hell.

"You didn't tell me this was a Greek party. Did you set me up?" I snapped at Jane.

"I'm sorry. I didn't know about this one. They didn't mention anything to me. Try to have fun anyway," Jane said apologetically.

"How can I enjoy myself if I will be breathing Nikos around here? This is torture. I'd rather leave, but I don't want to offend Curt and Robert."

"Hey, beautiful ladies, here's a shot of ouzo for you," Robert interrupted, handing each of us a shot glass of the deeply chilled Greek aperitif drink. I took the shot glass from his hand and swallowed the anise flavored liqueur.

"I think I will need more of this," I said, feeling the strong beverage heat my mouth and throat.

"Let me get you some more," Robert said, "in the meantime, please help yourselves. We ordered Greek appetizers from Bizantio, so go ahead and try everything on the table."

We approached the beautifully decorated table, filled with all sorts of Greek appetizers, but I wasn't hungry, much less for Greek food. Jane nibbled on some feta cheese and kalamata olives, while complimenting Curt on the decoration.

"So, you're really into your internship, right? Greek all the way?" Jane asked.

"Yes, of course, and I also wanted to honor our special guest today," Curt said.

"What special guest? Don't tell me…" Jane asked.

"Why, my darling, Dr. Nikos Soulis, who else could be our special Greek guest!" Curt exclaimed, visibly excited.

"You… you invited Nikos?" I gasped. Robert came back with another glass of ouzo and I snatched the drink from his hand, swallowing it in a straight shot.

"Not exactly… You see, I wanted to have a surprise party for him, sort of my way to say thanks because he's been so awesome during my internship in his department. He is just fabulous, isn't he?" Curt said.

"OK, Curt, so he doesn't know it's a party for him?" Jane asked, looking at me to gauge my reaction. I had asked Robert to bring me yet another shot of ouzo.

"I asked bitchy Maggie to bring him over, mind you!"

"You don't even like Maggie," Jane said, surprised.

"I don't, that's for sure. But what else could I do to bring him over to a surprise party? Only inviting the girlfriend… or whatever she is. She promised she would bring him over and I hope they're on their way."

"So Maggie is dating Nikos for sure?" Jane probed. I was speechless and Jane could tell I was in no condition to participate in the conversation.

"Let me fill you in… She told me she met him last year when she visited Greece with her father. So, I'm assuming that yes, they're dating," Curt said, excited about the gossip. That was some piece of information I had never heard of. So Maggie knew Nikos since last year, and he had never mentioned it to me. I felt wobbly. My head started to spin probably due to the three straight ouzo shots I drank, and I wanted to leave. Jane sensed my panic, coupled with my almost drunkenness. Robert put another shot glass of ouzo in my hand before being whisked away by Curt to chitchat with the other guests.

"Stop drinking like that," Jane said, "I think you've had enough. You need to eat something. You're getting drunk."

"I need to get out of here before he arrives with Maggie. This is a nightmare," I said before gulping down the ouzo shot.

"OK, let's get out of here. I'll take you home." As we were getting ready to leave, we heard the door bell. Curt looked through the peep hole and turned to all the guests inside, asking us to hush. When he opened the door, Nikos and Maggie were standing there, and everyone who had gathered closer to the entrance started clapping.

"Welcome, Dr. Soulis! Please enjoy this small token of appreciation in your honor," Curt said with excitement, gesturing for them to come inside. Nikos wore a crispy button down gray shirt and a pair of black trousers, while Maggie looked stunning in a pink silk dress and golden high heeled stilettos. I hated to admit it, but they looked gorgeous together. My heart sank. I needed to have another drink. After all, it was too painful for me to see them together like that. I escaped to the kitchen looking for the bottle of ouzo, while everyone greeted the couple. Jane followed me to the kitchen.

"What are you trying to do, get drunk in front of him?" she snapped at me.

"I can't handle this, Jane. It's unbearable. I'm so not over him yet, and seeing them together is killing me. I might as well turn myself over to Hades and die. I need to get out of here before he sees me, and yes, I need another drink, so I can pass out as soon as I get home."

"Stay cool. I know this looks like you pretty much walked into a trap and I'm very sorry. I had no idea Nikos would be here as a surprise guest of honor. All eyes are on Nikos and Maggie now. The main attraction has arrived, so no one will notice us leaving." Jane tried to calm me down. My legs were shaking. The anxiety I felt knowing Nikos and Maggie were in the house, combined with the alcohol I had already consumed were making me sick. I felt my face flushing and my heart beating faster. I just needed one more shot of ouzo before I left, so I grabbed a shot glass on the counter and filled it with the clear liquid from the bottle Robert had left on the table.

"Hey girls, look who's here," Curt said, entering the kitchen accompanied by Nikos. I gaped at him, not knowing what to do. My stomach felt queasy and my hands were shaking so violently that I spilled most of the ouzo from the shot glass I had just filled. Nikos stared at me with a somber expression, and his gaze fell on the glass I was holding. Jane looked at him and said hi, trying to sound casual so Curt wouldn't notice the awkwardness in the room.

"Let's have some drinks!" Curt exclaimed, while he filled two shot glasses of ouzo, offered one to Nikos and walked away with the other drink, looking for Maggie. Nikos placed his drink on the table, walked towards me and grabbed the half empty shot glass from my trembling hand.

He glanced at Jane. "How many shots did she have?"

"I'm not sure - four maybe," Jane said.

"I need another drink," I protested, trying to get my half empty glass back from Nikos.

"You're getting drunk. Have you eaten anything?" he asked.

I didn't respond. "She didn't eat anything. She's just drinking," Jane answered.

"This ouzo is very strong. You shouldn't be drinking it on an empty stomach. Eat something. You will feel better after you eat something," Nikos said.

"Just give me the damn drink. I don't want to eat anything."

"I'm taking you home. You're not drinking anything else tonight," he said in a serious tone.

"Nikos, leave her alone. I'll handle her," Jane intervened. "Do you realize she's like this because of you? And your presence here with Maggie doesn't help it."

"We need to talk," he said, looking at me and ignoring Jane. "Let me take you home so we can talk. You didn't let me finish what I had to say yesterday."

I gaped at him in disbelief, unable to comprehend his insistence in 'talking' to me, when it was so evident he and Maggie were in a relationship. He didn't make any sense and I didn't want to put myself in that fragile situation again, because I knew no matter what, once I was by myself with him, I wouldn't be able to resist his advances.

"No," I heard myself saying. "I have nothing else to talk to you about, Nikos."

"Please," Jane insisted, "can't you see you're hurting her even more? Leave Sabrina alone. Your girlfriend is here, go look for her."

Nikos looked at me and shook his head in resignation. "OK. I won't insist anymore. You know where to find me if you decide to let me talk to you." He faced Jane. "Please make sure you take her home and she eats something." He picked up the shot glass of ouzo Curt had handed to him a few moments earlier and walked out of the kitchen, bowing courteously to both of us. I was shaking uncontrollably and tried to fetch another drink, but Jane stopped me.

"No more drinks for you, girl. We're leaving now," she said, and holding me by the hand, Jane led me out of the house.

I was devastated. Never in my life had I ever thought I would fall in love so desperately with someone I barely knew, because these things only happen in fairly tales. This was one of those once in a lifetime feelings, a powerful, magical emotion hard to control, where both mind and heart were united into wanting one thing only: the object of my lust, the object of my passion, the object of my desire. Nikos was everything I had always dreamed of in a man, and he had been so close to my reach. My dream had become a reality for an evening, a few hours of unrelenting passion. And those memories were all I would ever have of the best night of my life.

Chapter 13

I dreaded going back to the museum on Monday. At least I had Sunday to recover from the shock of Curt and Robert's surprise party. As much as I didn't want to think about it, I couldn't help going over all that had happened the last couple of days, trying to make sense of it. Nikos had never told me he had known Maggie since the year before. It was strange how he avoided talking about her, and on the same token, Maggie sounded evasive every time Jane asked her anything about her relationship with Nikos. They definitely were trying to hide their romance, probably because of his personal policy of not getting involved with students and colleagues. What puzzled me was the fact he had flirted so openly with me - he made sure to cancel a previous engagement to have an afternoon talking to me about my project, he accepted going to the ballet with me on a Saturday night, he came to my apartment and made passionate love to me, and even after apologizing for what he had done, he still had kissed me ardently in his office a few days ago. It just didn't make sense, unless he was a real hypocrite who wanted to double date. Somehow I refused to believe this. The way he had looked at me, the way he had touched me, kissed me and loved me, it must have meant something to him. But what was my purpose in diving into this and trying to figure it out? I had to heal after all; my Greek god had been but an illusion.

A meeting with our University counselor had been scheduled for Monday evening, as it was time for all the interns to share their experiences and evaluate the program half way through the internship. Jane and I drove together from the museum to the University campus and met Curt and Robert there, along with the other six internship participants. I had to endure listening to Curt's non-stop worship of Nikos and the Antiquities curatorial department. He wouldn't stop raving about the project they were working on, and didn't spare compliments on Nikos' archaeological endeavors and museum knowledge. If Curt doesn't stop his adoration, Robert will end up jealous of Nikos, I reflected, amused by my inappropriate thought. The Greek god bewitched everyone and here was another one taken in by his irresistible charm. The counselor was obviously pleased with everyone's accounts of their experiences so far. When the meeting was over, the four of us stopped at La Madeleine on Rice Village for coffee and dessert.

"You girls disappeared from our Greek party the other night - what happened?" Robert asked, while sipping his cappuccino.

"Sabrina drank too much ouzo and was not feeling well," Jane said before I had a chance to respond, as usual. Sometimes her habit of chiming in and answer before me was annoying.

"I'm sorry, guys, the party was great but I miscalculated the power of the ouzo..." I said lightly. They all started laughing.

"Yes, we had a couple people also getting very drunk on it. We should have told everyone to eat before drinking," Robert said, taking a bite of his chocolate croissant.

"Yeah, Maggie, for example. She had way too many shots of ouzo and after a while, she was all over Nikos. She made him feel so uncomfortable. The guy doesn't seem to enjoy loving demonstrations of his private life in public, that's for sure," Curt told us.

"What happened?" Jane was curious.

"He kept apologizing for her behavior. She tried to kiss him and touch him inappropriately in front of everyone, and it was really embarrassing. Robert and I had to help him carry her downstairs to the car, because she was refusing to leave the party and Nikos wanted to take her home."

"I felt sorry for Nikos. I can't believe he was actually taking that crap from her so patiently. Maggie is totally obnoxious. I don't know what he sees in her," Robert said.

"I can imagine," Jane said with a smirk, "Maggie is very beautiful, and also very rich. You know her father is a huge benefactor of the museum, right?"

"Actually, Mr. Wallendorf is the main sponsor of the Greek Bronze Vessels exhibit. I found that out last week, when he came into the museum looking for Nikos. Cindy, our curator, thanked him in front of the whole staff for his contributions and for the success of the exhibit," Curt said.

"Why was Mr. Wallendorf looking for Nikos?" Jane asked. I was glad she was asking the questions. Even though I was curious about the story, I didn't want to seem the most eager one to know. I sipped my coffee and munched on the chocolate éclair I had ordered.

"Something to do with the Archaeological Museum in Athens where he works, I think," Curt responded. "He didn't say much to us. They went straight to Nikos' office and were there talking for probably an hour. I don't think Nikos was expecting his visit, though."

"Interesting to know. Maggie must be behind this. You said she went to Greece last year and that's when she met Nikos?" Jane asked.

Curt nodded. "That's what she said. She seems too comfortable around Nikos to have met him just a month ago. Their strange relationship has probably been going on for that long. But, as far as I can tell you, he doesn't feel at ease demonstrating their affair publicly."

"She's keeping him on a leash," Robert said, "she has his schedule, she's always on top of everything that's going on in his department, and she doesn't let him stray for a minute from his agenda. At first I thought she was just working as his secretary docent, but there's no way. Not after her demeanor in our party."

"And rumor has it that she's been watching every woman who spends too much time trying to get closer to him. By the way, you, my dear Sabrina," Curt said.

"Me what?" I gasped.

"Dr. Jones got you time with Nikos despite his busy schedule for you to work on your research, and Maggie was not happy about that when she found out."

"How do you know?" Jane asked.

"Maggie told me. She said she thought you were interested in him and that you were using your research to get closer to him," Curt said, eating the rest of his almond croissant.

"That bitch. She has no right to spread rumors," Jane said, defending me. "When did she tell you that?"

"When I told her about my surprise party for Nikos and asked her to bring him over. You know, we're not friends but I think she wanted to vent and found it was the right time to do so."

"What did you say? Did you fuel her rumors?" I asked, shaking inside. I hated the fact that Maggie was not being discreet about this situation, and throwing me under the bus by assuming my research was just a means to get closer to Nikos was very offensive.

"I told her you'd been working on that research way before Nikos arrived, and it was ridiculous of her to assume every woman who talked to Nikos was after him. Although he is a stud, the man is a Professor and he knows his stuff. There will always be lots of people after him: women and men!"

"Thanks, Curt. This is really disconcerting. I hope she's not going around telling everyone she thinks I'm using my research to seduce her boyfriend. That's not the case at all." I was frustrated. Not only did I have to deal with the hurt of knowing Nikos and Maggie had been together for a year, now I had to deal with Maggie's futile jealousy and defamation. My Greek god didn't descend from Olympus to seduce me; on the contrary, he descended from Olympus to cause mayhem.

"Well, girls, we're going home. I'm helping Nikos with a presentation tomorrow for curators from the Atlanta Museum. They are interested in hosting the Greek vases, and I need to go over it tonight. It's all about Greece," Curt said, laughing, and both he and Robert excused themselves and left the restaurant.

"And the plot thickens..." Jane said when the guys were gone.

"I don't know what to make of all of this, really. I'm confused."

"Who wouldn't be? This whole thing doesn't make much sense. I can't believe how embarrassing for Nikos it might have been when Maggie got drunk and tried to touch and kiss him in front of everyone. He deserves that!" Jane said.

"I'm glad I was gone. That would have been sickening to see."

"What was he thinking when he came to your place and made love to you? I hate to think that he used you. It sucks. He's a player, and Maggie's behavior serves him right. I hope she creates more scandalous scenes for him before he leaves," Jane exclaimed.

"There is something going on with Mr. Wallendorf, though. The last time I saw Nikos, he got lots of calls from Greece and he didn't seem to be very happy on the phone. When Maggie called, he mentioned something about her father. Maybe he's trying to get a sponsorship for his museum from Mr. Wallendorf's philanthropic organization."

"And Mr. Wallendorf came to the museum to talk to him. I'll try to find out more about it, but you should stay as far from the commotion as possible."

"Definitely. The farther away I am from Maggie the better," I said.

"And from Nikos too, don't forget," Jane completed.

I frowned, although I knew she was right. My whole being ached for Nikos, but I knew I had to keep this longing in check. Avoiding Nikos was the best course of action to prevent more heartache.

****

My project was going great and I was delighted that the redesigning of the African gallery was on time. The department was planning the grand opening by the end of the month as expected, despite some hiccups with the size of some of the displays. The curator had asked me to take two pieces back to the storage room, located on the lower level of the museum, which was inaccessible to visitors. The storage room had to be kept locked at all times, and there was usually no one around the hallway leading to it, except for a security guard by the elevator door who kept the key to open the area. For security reasons, the museum allowed only two workers inside the storage room at a time, and the security officer had to keep a log on the computer to make a notation of the employee number, time of entry, time of exit and what object was either removed or put back in storage.

I showed the security officer my badge and the two artifacts I was going to store back from the African gallery. The friendly, lonely guy typed the information carefully before unlocking the door for me. The room was cold and loaded with boxes and containers that were acclimated to keep relics and other valuable art pieces and antiquities from damage while they were not being exhibited to the public. I had to find the shelf that held the African collection and catalog the two objects accurately. Since I had been to the storage room once to retrieve a golden African mask, I was somewhat familiar with the location of the African collection. I found the shelf and removed the boxes, being careful not to drop or bump into anything. While I was performing my meticulous task, I heard the door open and close. A second person had just come into the storage room. However, I didn't take much notice of it and continued doing my job, as it was very common for two curators to be at the storage room at the same time. I finished storing the objects and sat at the desk to type the names and numbers of the pieces on the computer log, when I heard unhurried steps coming in my direction. It must be the curator, I thought, she might have forgotten to give me something else to store.

"Hi, Sabrina," I heard a familiar yet sensual voice whisper my name. I looked up thinking I was dreaming but to my utter despair, Nikos was standing in front of me. My heart almost stopped beating, and I was glad I had already placed the antique objects inside the boxes, or I might have dropped them. I jumped from the chair as if I had seen a ghost.

"I'm sorry, I didn't mean to scare you," he said in a low voice.

"What are you doing here?" I murmured.

"I work here too, remember?" He smirked. "I need to get an object for the Greek gallery. But I read the security officer's log and saw someone was here storing African objects. It crossed my mind it might be you."

I gasped and felt my heart speeding up. Why was he coming to see if it was I who was in the room? Why did he insist on hurting my feelings? Was he that cruel? After all, he knew what he did to me.

"And I'm glad I was right. It is you," he continued.

"What do you want?" I asked with my barely audible voice.

"Why are you avoiding me?"

"Nikos, you know why I'm avoiding you. Don't do this to me. Why are you insisting in doing this?"

"You don't know what is going on and you're running away from me without giving me a chance to talk to you. Why am I doing what? I just want to talk to you and clarify some misunderstandings. And you won't let me."

"What misunderstandings? That you went to bed with me and you shouldn't because you have been dating Maggie for a year? I get that."

"When are you all going to stop with this nonsense that I'm dating Maggie? It's you, and your friend Jane, and then Curt and Robert and their idea of a surprise party for me, involving Maggie to secretly bring me over to their place... I don't know where else this is escalating to."

I stared at him in disbelief - how could he deny his affair with Maggie so bluntly?

"I can't believe you're trying to hide your relationship with her. You really are a hypocrite. I know you met her last year in Athens and you've been dating her since. She's been guarding you like a treasure since you arrived here. She's like your shadow, everywhere you go she's just behind you. And everyone saw her at Curt's party."

"Saw what? That she got drunk and behaved like an idiotic teenager?" Nikos asked, pacing the floor as if he was Minotaur waiting for his prey.

I sighed. "Look, don't try to deny it. She confronted me. She told me to back off and stop going after you with my poor excuse of a research paper," I muttered, looking down at the floor. The situation with Maggie had been upsetting.

Nikos stopped pacing and stepped closer to me. "Maggie did what?" His penetrating, dark eyes conveyed a menacing look, but I could tell his anger was not directed towards me. I looked away from him and stared again at the floor.

"Maggie told me you are her boyfriend and she didn't appreciate me trying to get closer to you by using my research paper as an excuse. And she's not making a secret of it either," I reiterated.

Nikos walked away from me shaking his head, and ran his fingers nervously through his hair. He turned around again to face me, put his hands in his jeans pockets and inhaled deeply. "What did you say to her?" His voice was calm and calculated, he had quickly recomposed himself.

I glanced back at him. "I told her I was not after you and my research was the only reason I had to talk to you… and if I needed to get your assistance I would…"

"Is it true?" he asked.

"Yes, of course. I needed help with my research and you were kind enough to…"

He didn't let me finish it. "Is it true that your research was the only reason you needed to see me?"

I felt chills running through my spine. He was too close for comfort and I desperately wanted to tell him that no, it was not true; of course my research was not the only reason I needed him. Oh Nikos, can't you see what you do to me? Can't you see I'm hopelessly in love with you? Can't you see how much I hurt from thinking you and Maggie are together? I needed the strength to tell him it was true, that I didn't want him for nothing but my research paper, but I knew he would be able to see through my lie. I was trapped in Minotaur's labyrinth, no matter what I said. Nikos was waiting patiently for my answer. But I avoided his eyes, debating in my thoughts what to say, and how not to betray myself once more. Feeling my hesitation, he stepped closer to me and lifted my head with his hands, staring intently into my eyes, looking into my soul as if I was an oracle and he was attempting to read me. I tried to free my head from his hands, but his grip got stronger and he didn't let me move. I was almost burning with the heat of his body inches away from me. I was, once again, a prisoner of his charm. Nikos was too irresistible and I had no strength to fight him.

"Is it true?" he insisted with his husky, sexy voice. I felt his sweet breath on my face. He was too dangerously close to me.

"What do you think?" I managed to whisper. Nikos didn't answer. His mouth closed in on mine, forcing my lips open with his tongue, entering my mouth without boundaries, sucking the breath out of me, filling me with an indescribable desire and satiating my hunger momentarily. His fierce kiss grew in intensity and I felt him growing underneath his jeans, getting harder as he pressed on my leg. It was too much to bear. It was starting all over again and I knew exactly where it would end. Nowhere. I thought about what Curt had said, and the image of a drunken Maggie kissing Nikos and touching him during the party came to my mind. I pushed him away from me.

"Stop it, Nikos. Don't do this to me again," I begged. He released me, looking confused.

"I know you want me, Sabrina. You want me as much as I want you, don't you?"

I was exasperated. "Of course I want you, but I can't let you do this to me, Nikos, not while you're dating Maggie and… and then what? You go back to Greece. And what about me? What do I mean to you, just a sex adventure? I have feelings, I can't… I can't let you do this to me." I was on the verge of tears. My cell phone buzzed, signaling the arrival of a text message. I pulled the phone from my pocket to read the message and realized suddenly I had been in the storage room much longer than needed. The text was from my curator, asking me if I had found the location and if the pieces had been stored appropriately.

"I need to go, the curator is looking for me," I said, as I typed a quick text back to let her know I was on my way. Nikos looked at me and nodded.

"Can I invite you for coffee after work today?" he asked.

"Nikos, I… I don't think it's a good idea. I can't do it today, anyway."

"Look, Sabrina. I just want to talk to you. We can go to Starbucks or another coffee shop and I promise you I won't touch you or make you feel uncomfortable. I really want to talk to you and tell you my side of the story. I mean it. Give me a chance." He sounded so truthful.

"Maybe tomorrow…" I mumbled.

"Call me tomorrow, then, or text me to confirm. We can go straight from here in my car and I'll drop you back."

"I will," I said, leaving Nikos behind in the storage area. I opened the heavy door of the storage room, which could only be opened without a key from the inside, and walked towards the security guard who was sitting comfortably at his desk, playing a game on his cell phone. He entered the time I was exiting on his log and I got into the elevator to go back up to my department.

I had no idea why I had agreed to have coffee with Nikos. It was just another delay in trying to close the chapter of my frustrated love story. What else could he say to me? Would he insist there was nothing between Maggie and him? That he wanted me as much as I wanted him? Or apologize again for seducing me? I shook my head and sighed. It was his last chance. I would allow him to say whatever it was he wanted to say to me and then I would hopefully be on my way to healing from his spell. I stepped out of the elevator and walked towards the African gallery, checking my messages on the phone, when, to my dismay, I ran into Maggie. She was walking in my direction and stopped in front of me, obstructing my way.

"Have you seen Nikos?" she asked me directly, not bothering to greet me.

"Did you lose your boyfriend?" I smirked. My dislike for Maggie was growing exponentially every time I saw her or heard of her.

She looked at me with a condescending expression. "Don't mess with me, Sabrina. I know you're after him," she said.

"You're wrong, Maggie. I have work to do and no time to fool around like you. And I'd appreciate it if you would stop spreading rumors about Nikos and I. And no, I haven't seen him. Happy?"

Maggie snorted and moved out of my way, walking firmly towards the opposite direction. I wished I had told her that her boyfriend and I had been kissing in the storage room downstairs. I'd love to see her indignant expression.

Chapter 14

Nikos was waiting for me at the Starbucks on West Gray. I had texted him earlier to tell him I would meet him there. It was better for us to drive in separate cars, in case our conversation didn't end on a good note. I loved the West Gray Starbucks. Rodney, the barista, knew me and he prepared the best mocha Frappuccino in the city. Nikos ordered an espresso, which seemed to be his favorite coffee drink, while Rodney confirmed whether I wanted whipped cream on top of my cold drink. I smiled and nodded. We sat by the window on a small side table facing the parking lot with our drinks. Up to now, Nikos hadn't said anything except when he had greeted me. I was in a familiar territory; a place I even knew the employees, which gave me a little bit of protection from the god of love, from this Eros I was so afraid of. Nikos took a sip of his hot coffee, his eyes observing me with intensity.

"Thank you for agreeing to see me."

I gave him an acknowledging smile, while I slurped the frothy whipped cream from my Frappuccino. "How are you doing?" he asked.

"Not bad. Lots of hard work coming to an end, and it's good to see the great results. You know we're reopening the African Arts gallery at the end of the month, right? Everything is on schedule," I said, trying to keep the conversation on a professional level.

"That's great," he said. "I hear you're doing a wonderful job with the redesigning. Are you done with your research paper yet?"

"No. I've been so busy I decided to take a break from it. You gave me enough guidance and materials and I feel comfortable with what I have."

"You know you can always reach out to me if you need help with it or with anything else. I hope you don't forget I exist when I go back to Greece." His eyes were barely blinking, and he spoke in an almost sad tone, as if this was the last conversation we were having, like a farewell. I felt my heart sinking, for I still longed for him so much and it was hard to be so close to him and pretend we were just colleagues. And the prospect of him leaving soon to go back to Greece was an awful feeling. The museum would never be the same without him, and I was already feeling like Calypso, abandoned by her lover Ulysses, who continued on his search to go home to Penelope.

"No," I said, "I will not forget you exist. How could I? Everything in the museum will remind me of you. Every Greek artifact will have been found by you. Every Greek restaurant will have your taste." He gave me his sexy faint smile. His phone buzzed. He picked it up, read the message, but didn't reply. I couldn't help asking about it.

"Is it Maggie looking for you?" His expression darkened.

"No more jokes about it, please." He sounded serious and wasn't amused at all that I had mentioned Maggie when he received the text.

"I'm sorry," I said. "I couldn't help it. She usually seems to show up every time I am close to you."

"Maggie and I met last year," Nikos started. "She and her father were touring some European museums and they ended up in Athens. I had just gotten my PhD and was promoted to my current position as assistant director of the Antiquities department. Mr. Wallendorf was very interested in meeting me, because he had heard about some of my archaeological findings and wanted to purchase an item I had excavated, for his personal collection." He took another sip of his espresso and waited for me to say something. I just nodded for him to continue.

"Our museum couldn't sell him the item. It was an artifact of cultural significance and since it was found in Greek soil, it belongs to the Greek museum. But Mr. Wallendorf was intent in demonstrating his charitable interest, so he himself proposed the idea of putting the Greek Bronze Vessel exhibit together to bring it to Houston. We worked on a plan and he was thrilled to help sponsor the project. But our museum is still facing financial problems because of the current economic situation."

"I'm sorry to hear about the financial difficulties the museum is having. I hope there's a way to get funds," I said, remembering what he had told me before about finding investors and benefactors. "But you don't owe me all this explanation, Nikos. Really, you owe me nothing."

He finished his espresso. "I want to tell you what is going on. I don't want you assuming things because you're hearing gossips or seeing things you don't understand."

"Why is it so important for you to tell me all of this?"

"Because I don't want you to have the wrong impression of me, after what happened with us."

I shook my head. "We had a rough start, Nikos... I don't know what to think..." I said pensively.

"Let me continue, and then you see if you can understand and forgive me." Nikos continued with his explanation. Mr. Wallendorf was interested in investing in the museum, but with the current economic situation, foreign investors were being swayed into investing in big corporations, and anything related to arts or non-profit organizations were not allowed to receive grants for the time being. Nikos was trying to bring the exhibit to other museums in North America, in hopes of securing enough funds to reopen some of the museum's galleries, but bureaucracy was delaying the negotiations. He had already met with the director of the Atlanta museum, and the Chicago museum's director was coming the following week. He also was in negotiations to loan some pieces of the Greek Vessel exhibit to other museums in the country, and those discussions were getting the red tape from the Ministry of Culture in Greece. And that's one of the reasons he was receiving so many calls from his associates during the night.

"I really hope you can make things work," I said. "I can certainly understand you're under a lot of pressure."

"Yes, thank you. Mr. Wallendorf has been of great help. He is really trying to move mountains to help us out. He wants Maggie to become a more active participant in his philanthropic organization and asked her to oversee the programs and projects we're involved with."

"Are you telling me Maggie is a business partner of sorts?" I asked, curious.

"Yes, sort of. She took an interest in it after she visited the museum last year."

"Because of you?" I imagined Maggie falling head over heels for this Greek god and pestering her father to help him.

"It could be. I'm not sure. But I don't really care why. She's elated that her father has given her this project to manage. And as you can see, she's been trying hard to keep up with it."

"To keep up with *you*," I corrected him. "Are you trying to convince me there's nothing between you and Maggie but a business relationship?"

"No. I'm not trying to convince you of anything. I'm telling you why Maggie is involved with me at this point."

"Are you... are you sleeping with her? I mean, she goes around saying you're her boyfriend, and..."

"I'm not sleeping with her, despite what you may have heard."

"Have you slept with her before? Did you have an affair with her when she was in Greece? It's just that... somehow she seems so comfortable talking about you and..."

"Why are you asking me these questions? What difference does it make whatever happened in the past?" Nikos asked me, staring deeply into my eyes.

"You have, haven't you? I knew it... You have slept with Maggie, haven't you?" I insisted.

He took his eyes off me, looked out the window and sighed. "If it makes you feel better, yes, I have. I slept with her in Greece a year ago. One time, one mistake, one bad judgment on my part." I felt nauseous and my heart sank. I was sure something had happened or was happening between them, but I had no idea I was going to feel so upset when I heard it from him. I was heavy with jealousy.

"Am I also a one time, one mistake, and one bad judgment on your part?" I mumbled, shaking.

Nikos gaped at me. "No, you're not." He reached for my hand that was resting on the table next to my almost empty Frappuccino cup and held it softly. My instincts were telling

97

me to pull it back but I couldn't move and I let his strong, masculine hand rest on mine. "You're not a mistake, Sabrina, and I'd love to get to know you better, if we only had the time on our side."

I couldn't believe he said that. My heart was pounding so hard I could feel it through my blouse. My mouth was dry. I grabbed the Frappuccino cup with my free hand and sipped the rest of the cold milky liquid through the green straw without taking my eyes off him. The whirlwind of emotions was at play once more. I was unable to resist him, and melted under his hot gaze. The spell was not broken and I was Leda, about to be seduced by Zeus disguised as a swan.

"Let's get out of here," he said suddenly. Nikos grabbed my hand and led me out of Starbucks without saying a word. He opened the door to his car, I got in without questions, and we drove off. I had no idea what his intentions were, where he wanted to take me or what he wanted to do, except that I was overjoyed because I was with him. There was nothing I could do: I was totally smitten by him. He held my hand tenderly and brushed it against his lip. His soft, loving kiss was all I needed to be on fire again. I glanced at him, surprised by his gentleness. Still holding my hand he asked, "Do you believe me?" I nodded and mumbled a faint yes. "Do you want to be with me tonight?" he asked.

I turned to him, stunned by his question. He kept his eyes on the road, still holding my hand. "Yes," I answered. "I want to be with you." He kissed my hand again before releasing it, and didn't say anything else until he parked the car in front of his luxury apartment complex.

We got out of the car and walked inside his apartment. It looked like a hotel room; there was nothing personal about a furnished rental, and he made no effort to customize the place, which was spotless. A comfortable black leather sofa was the main furniture in the spacious living room, and a matching chair stood next to it. A half empty book shelf stood by the wall next to a window overlooking the parking lot. On the coffee table, a glass vase with cut stalks of a Lucky Bamboo plant was the only decoration.

Nikos walked to the kitchen while I waited in the living room, and offered me a glass of water. I was nervous again, alone with Nikos in his apartment, realizing he was a man I still didn't know much about, and with whom I was totally infatuated. He came back to the living room holding two glasses of cold water.

"Make yourself comfortable," he said. "And thank you for being here with me." He sat on the sofa and drank his water, all the while staring at me. I sat on the chair opposite from him. There were so many things I wanted to ask him, so many things I wanted to know about him, but I didn't know where to start. The way he looked at me still intimidated me.

"You're welcome. I'm glad you enjoy my company," I said timidly. His cell phone vibrated, he pulled it out of his pocket to check who was calling and frowned. He typed a few words, silenced it and placed it on top of the side table next to the sofa, letting out a sigh.

"I won't to lie to you. That was Maggie, looking for me, but I told her I was busy tonight."

"I don't want to cause problems for you. I know you need Maggie to help you out with your negotiations and the last thing I want is to prevent it from happening because of me. If it's better for me to leave..." I said.

"No, please. I want you to be here with me. I want to take my mind off work, and Maggie, and all this crazy business... Look, Sabrina, I don't want you to think I brought you here for sex. I'm attracted to you, of course I am, and I'd love to make love to you again but I don't want you to think I'm using you. I want you to believe me first. I don't want to hurt your feelings. I don't want to cause you pain."

"I don't know what to think, Nikos. Part of me wants to believe you, but part of me is signaling for me to run. The way Maggie talks about you in such a possessive, jealous, controlling way... it makes it hard for me to believe there's nothing going on between the two of you." My mind was going around in circles. Why did I let myself be carried away by him again? I should have known better this was not going to end well for me. Now I knew Maggie was behind him to help his museum financially, and that was huge. If she wanted him, she was going to do all she could to have him, and I stood no chance against her. There was no help I could offer Nikos to save his museum or his job. And he had slept with her, which weighed heavily on my heart. Did he make love to her the same way he made love to me? I couldn't bear to think about that. It hurt so much to imagine Nikos kissing and loving Maggie the way he had done to me not long ago. I was completely lost, setting myself up for more heartbreak. Why couldn't I say no to him?

"I've told Maggie that what happened between us last year is not going to happen again. It was a mistake. That night, we had dinner with her father and he had given me the great news about the project's approval. I was excited about it and ended up drinking more than I should. Maggie invited me to her hotel room and it happened. I was half drunk. I should have controlled myself," Nikos explained.

"Maggie is a pretty woman. I'm sure you had a hard time resisting her. Why didn't it work out between you two?"

"Yes, Maggie is a very beautiful woman but that's not what matters to me. She has a suffocating personality. She's very demanding, and she doesn't have a genuine interest in the arts. It's all because of her father's influence, but I don't feel it is her passion. Unlike you."

"Unlike me?" I asked. "But you don't know much about me..."

"I know enough. You love the same things I love. I can see it in your eyes when you talk about Greek art, how you're really passionate about it. I sensed it the first time I saw you at the opening of the exhibit. The way you looked at the Greek vase and how you talked about it. I was immediately drawn to you." I was speechless, I had no idea Nikos had observed me that well. "That's why I was willing to meet with you and help you with your project, and Dr. Jones was more than happy to accommodate my request. Maggie was supposed to take me out that afternoon, and she was not very happy when Dr. Jones canceled the engagement."

"I don't know what to say. You surprise me," I said softly. Oh my Olympian god, how much I want to be in your arms right now.

"Maggie volunteered to be a docent because that's the only way she could get unlimited access to me. Even though her father is one of the main benefactors of the museum, there are some guidelines and she can't just walk in and out as she pleases. So Dr. Jones gave her the assignment to be sort of my assistant while she volunteered as a docent," Nikos explained. So that's why Maggie was going around driving him and keeping tabs on his schedules, meetings, etc. It was going to be very hard to get her out of the way, especially since she correctly assumed I was interested in Nikos.

"Is Maggie the reason you didn't want me telling anyone we went to the ballet?"

"I really don't go out with students and colleagues. A lot of students and museum personnel have been inviting me out to show me the city; or to go to a particular restaurant or show, but I decline all of them. I didn't want any rumors spreading about you and me going out, for your sake," Nikos justified. I nodded. I was still confused about the situation. Regardless of what Nikos said, our relationship was doomed to end, although it had barely started. In a few weeks, he was to return to Greece, and I would go back to school and to my work as an art teacher. The museum adventure was about to be over soon, and Nikos and Maggie were going to be working together under her father's sponsorship. I had to think about what I really wanted. Another hot night with Eros, my god of love and sex? Or should I just keep whatever happened between us as a wonderful souvenir and run from more heartache?

I wanted to run, but I had no strength to flee. Staring at Nikos, I knew I was going to surrender. That's all I'd been wanting for the last couple of days. The furtive encounters we had, kissing, touching and not going further because of the interruptions and obstacles we faced, had left me wanting him even more. And now I had the opportunity to spend the whole night with him, in his place, and have the most unforgettable time of my life, again. It might be the last time, too. Nikos broke the silence.

"So…aren't you going to say something, or ask me anything?"

"I don't know what to think. You have to go back to Greece and… I mean, it's… complicated," I said, getting up to take the empty water glass back to the kitchen. He followed me.

"Do you want to leave?" he asked. I placed the glass on the kitchen counter and turned to face him. He was right behind me, also holding his empty glass. I looked straight into his dark, expressive eyes.

"No," I said, and wrapped my arms around his neck, lifting my lips to touch his. Surprised with my reaction, Nikos put his glass on the counter and enveloped me with his strong arms, opening his mouth to receive my kiss. His delicious taste inebriated me, and my body got closer to his, while our mouths continued to savor each other, fueling a passion so hard to restrain. I moved my hands to his chest to unbutton his shirt, and revealed his impeccably sculpted abs, firm and absolutely statuesque physique. I wanted him more than anything. His shirt fell to the floor, and he raised me up gently to place me on top of the kitchen counter, lifting my blouse over my head and letting it fall on the floor next to his shirt. Just like the last time he had tried to undress me while we were in his office in the museum, he swiftly unfastened my bra to expose my hardened nipples. While he held me in his arms over the kitchen counter, his wet tongue slid gently down my neck, finding its way to my right nipple, and moved in circles around it, causing a rousing sensation down my spine and wakening the fountain inside of me. I moaned in pleasure, unable to contain my excitement. His lips moved fast, nibbling and sucking my nipples, alternating between the right and the left, ensuring they remained firm as plump cherries. I held on lightly to his head, moving my fingers to comb his deliciously fragrant and luscious dark hair, while I wrapped my legs around his waist.

My handsome Eros moved his mouth up to mine again and kissed me with implacable passion, leaving me breathless. He picked me up while my legs were still wrapped around him and took me to the bedroom, laying me delicately on the huge king size bed. I looked at him with fire in my eyes, yearning for him to touch me and kiss me again. He climbed on top of me, lifting my arms and pinning me down under his sculptured body, lowering his head to kiss my mouth again. I wriggled under his weight, moving my hips to accommodate him in-between my legs. He released my arms and moved his hands and mouth down to my nipples again, licking me all the way down to my navel. His hands moved speedily to my jeans, unzipping them and discarding the rest of the clothing that covered my body on the floor. My skin tingled under his seductive and sexy gaze, as he backed away from me to unbutton his own pants and remove the rest of his clothes.

He was hard and ready to penetrate me, but instead of entering me, he kissed my navel again, holding my hips with both his hands, his fingers moving down in a firm caress. I moaned in anticipation of his lips on me and arched my back, lifting my hips and opening my legs. Nikos kissed me softly on my most intimate part, and his wet tongue started to explore and move with steady and firm movements, driving me insane with pleasure while I grabbed on to his hair, waiting to explode in ecstasy. It didn't take long for my soft moans to turn into a loud sigh of pleasure as I couldn't hold his teasing any longer. I quivered in blissful anguish while my body relaxed on the bed. Nikos climbed up next to me to caress my face. My heart was still beating furiously and my chest heaved with my fast breathing. I looked at his loving eyes and smiled. I can spend the rest of my life here with you, my Greek hero, I thought.

"How are you feeling, my beautiful goddess?" he asked.

"I'm feeling like Helen of Troy, Paris, my hero. You're just amazing," I answered. "You drive me crazy."

He smirked and stroked my hair, lying next to me. I moved on top of him and kissed his mouth. It was my turn to please my Greek god. I bit his lips lightly and moved my mouth to nibble on his earlobe, blowing softly on his ear. My tongue descended to his neck and chest, and I licked his body with long, wet strides, delighting in his luscious and masculine scent that turned me on so much. His body was a beautiful temple. He looked as if he had been sculptured from a rare Costa Sol bronze marble block, and transformed into this perfect specimen of a man. Yes, bronze marble for sure, a word derived from the Greek - mármaros, which meant a crystalline rock or shining stone. My beautiful god made of shining stone. How could I keep myself from loving you when everything I think of reminds me of you?

My hand touched him, and I opened my mouth to taste him, closing my lips firmly on the hardened object of my desire. Moving my head in an incessant motion with my tongue going up and down, I swallowed his length all the way while my fingers caressed him tenderly. I sucked him tightly, applying an even pressure and keeping him all the way inside my mouth. After a while, he suddenly pulled me in to him, lifting me with his strong hands and placing me carefully on top of him. I felt him sliding inside of me without resistance. I rode on top of him, wildly, feeling him so hard and ready inside, burning me with desire. I knew I could spend the rest of the night taking him, having him inside of me, loving him so ardently. While he held on to my hips as I moved steadily on top of him, I lowered my face to touch his mouth again, and we kissed with carelessly abandon, as if there was nothing else in the world at that moment, just the two of us, two bodies squirming in passion, trying to satiate a powerful and uninhibited desire. I finally felt him exploding inside of me, as he gripped my hips and pressured me down further onto him. I squeezed his arms, shuddering with the thrilling sensation of his release.

Satisfied and exhausted, I lied down next to him. Nikos opened his arms and I cuddled inside his protective, warm embrace. "I want to be with you forever," I whispered. He stared at me with loving eyes and kissed my forehead while caressing my hair, but didn't say anything. He moved to kiss my mouth again, and I wasn't surprised to feel him growing once more pressed to my leg. I knew it was going to be a long and memorable night next to my Greek stud.

****

I don't know how many times we made love during the night, but at some point I drifted off to sleep, worn out and

104

completely exhausted. When I woke up, I was still in his arms, and the sun was shining through the blinds, illuminating the Greek god next to me. I kissed him lightly on his lips. Nikos opened his eyes and rubbed them, trying to shield away from the sunlight.

"What time is it?" I asked him. There were no clocks in the bedroom and both our cell phones had been left unattended in the living room since last night. He jumped out of bed all of a sudden and walked fast to the living room.

"Oh, no," I heard him. "We're late. It's almost 9 am. I can't believe I overslept. It never happens to me." I jumped out of the bed and joined him in the living room, reaching for my cell phone. There were already a bunch of missed calls and texts.

I looked at him, feeling totally guilty. "I'm sorry, it's my fault. I shouldn't have come," I said. Nikos moved closer and put his arms around me.

"It's OK, my goddess," he said gently, kissing me on the forehead. "Let's get dressed. I'll drop you at Starbucks and you can drive your car. We don't want to arrive at the museum late together," he said. I gave him a quick kiss on his lips and walked into the kitchen to pick up the rest of my clothes still lying on the floor. While Nikos took a shower, I got dressed quickly, scanned my missed calls and texts, and called in to the museum to talk to my manager.

"I'm so sorry I haven't called you earlier, but I'm having car problems. I should be there in about an hour," I gave her a lame excuse, but she understood and accepted it. I knew I would have a harder time lying to Jane, though. She had left several messages and texts trying to find out where I was. I would have to deal with her later, but in order to prevent further calls, I sent her a text to let her know I was alive and would be coming in to the museum later that morning. Nikos got out of the shower, dropped the towel on the bed and walked in naked towards the closet to choose something to wear. I let out a sigh upon seeing him. I couldn't help admiring his absolutely perfect body, and I also noticed he was hard again.

"You don't want to take a quick shower?" he asked, glancing at me and noticing I was already dressed.

"I'll stop home before driving to the museum. I don't want you to be even later than you already are," I said, trying to avoid staring at his body. Just looking at his magnificent hardened body was making me wet again. He chose a light green polo shirt and a pair of khakis and dressed in front of me.

"Are you going to be OK? Have you notified your supervisor you're running late?" he asked, while zipping up his pants. Nikos was a feast for my eyes.

"Yes…yes, I called and said I'm having car trouble, but I'm worried about you. What are you going to say?" I asked.

"Don't worry, I'll think of something. I had an appointment this morning with Curt and the team that's working with me to go over their project, but if I need to, I will see them after hours later today."

"What about Maggie?" I asked.

"What *about* Maggie?" he repeated back to me.

"You know, she's the keeper of your schedule. I'm surprised she hasn't come knocking at your door yet," I smirked.

"As a matter of fact, she is on her way here," he said nonchalantly. I gaped at him.

"Are you kidding me?"

"She sent me a text about five minutes ago letting me know she was coming over to see if I was home, since I haven't answered the phone or her texts and haven't shown up for my meeting yet," he said calmly, walking back to the bathroom to comb his hair and brush his teeth. I couldn't believe he was acting so relaxed. Maggie was on her way to his place. What if she found me in here? I stood perplexed, waiting for him. Nikos emerged out of the bathroom ready to go. He picked up his keys from the table, put his cell phone in his pocket and opened the door for me.

"Let's go, goddess," he said, and I promptly exited the apartment. We walked to the parking lot and I quickly got inside his car. "Don't worry," he said, holding my hand. "She has to go through the security guard at the entrance. If they call me and there's no answer, she can't drive in. I will exit using the back residents' entrance," he calmly explained. I sighed in relief, happy we were avoiding a possible encounter that surely would result in a scandalous scene from Maggie.

Chapter 15

By the time I arrived at the museum, it was almost at noon. I hadn't eaten anything yet and was starving, so after checking in at my department and getting my assignments for the afternoon, I was glad to go to lunch. My tardiness didn't have a big impact on my projects. I had done enough the day before and was still on schedule. Jane was waiting for me at Café Express. The place was full and we stood in line to order our food.

"OK, Miss M.I.A., where have you been all evening and this morning?" she asked as soon as she saw me, without even saying hello. I grinned.

"Do you really want to know?"

"Oh, no, don't tell me. By your naughty grin, I can guess, but I just can't believe it. It smells Greek to me," she said. "Really?"

"Well, you don't want me to tell you, do you?" I teased her.

"Every detail, in full color," she answered. The cashier rang our order and gave us the pager to let us know when our food was ready. We chose a quiet table at the back of the restaurant to chat without all the lunch noise around us. I filled my glass with water while Jane got some croutons and olives from the Oasis bar.

"So, are you the reason Greek god was not here earlier this morning and bitchy Maggie was going insane looking for him in all departments?" Jane asked as soon as we sat at the table. I nodded.

"She was about to call the police, thinking he was involved in an accident or something. She was totally out of control," Jane continued.

"Are you serious?"

"Yes, and get ready to take on her fury. Crazy Medusa found out you were not here either and her anxiety grew. She wanted me to get a hold of you like, yesterday."

"And what did you say?"

"I told her I'm not your mother and if you were late to come to work, you had your reasons, and how it was ridiculous of her to assume something like that. So, she sort of came to her senses temporarily and buzzed off."

"She's unbelievable..." I muttered.

"And there's more. Curt told me she brought Dr. Jones up to the Antiquities department and wanted him to question everyone about Nikos' whereabouts. When Dr. Jones realized what she was doing, he told her Nikos was a grown man and didn't need a babysitter, and if he was not there yet, he might have a good reason for it. She was ridiculous, it was just like 9:30 am, and I think he showed up close to 10:30. I mean, he wasn't even *that* late. The woman is a basket case," Jane laughed.

"Yeah, of course, both of us being late on the same day is going to make her very suspicious."

"What is going on between the two of you now? Seriously, what happened?" Jane frowned, putting on a serious expression on her face.

"He told me he's not dating Maggie."

"And do you believe him, you foolish girl in love?"

"Come on, Jane, give him a chance. Why would he lie?" I asked.

"Why wouldn't he lie? If he can have both of you, why wouldn't he lie? Besides, he's going back to Greece in a few more weeks, so why wouldn't he have fun?" Jane asked.

I shook my head. "No, he's not like that," I said.

"If you want to be heartbroken, that's your problem. Don't tell me later I didn't advise you. Nikos is bad news, especially with Maggie as his shadow."

"He told me he slept with her, though. He didn't lie about that. Once. Last year in Greece, when they met. Her father is interested in being an investor, but Maggie is the liaison for all the philanthropic projects concerning the museum where he works. That's why she's so involved with him," I explained.

Jane sighed. "I still don't believe him. Maggie is way too involved with *him*, not with his museum. That's the behavior of a lover, not of a business partner."

"Jane, I have been waiting for Nikos since I read the first chapter of the Iliad." I said. "I can't resist him. I'm very drawn to him. When we're together, it's magical."

"Do you know what his last name means?"

"Did you look it up?"

"Let's say I just happened on it. It means *unexplained* and there are a lot of unexplained things in Nikos' story. I know you're really lost in Olympus but I hope your hero is a real one, not a fake." The pager buzzed and Jane got up to get our lunch. I waited for her at the table, watching museum patrons and employees come and go, thinking about Maggie's reaction when she couldn't get a hold of Nikos during the morning.

"Hello, my sweetie, can I join you?" Curt said, awakening me from my daydreams.

"Sure, please, take a seat. Jane is coming back with our plates," I said.

Curt pulled out one of the chairs and sat down with his salad bowl and a glass of iced tea. Jane returned, bringing in our sandwiches, and was thrilled to find Curt at our table.

"OK girls, you know how I hate gossip, but I have to tell you this one," Curt said excitedly.

"Oh, it must be something good then," Jane joked. We all knew Curt loved a good gossip and he was usually the first one to know all the interesting rumors. I'm glad he hadn't picked up on my relationship with Nikos yet. Maybe he sensed something, but since he really liked me and was totally in awe of Nikos, I hadn't heard anything nasty coming from him regarding the two of us.

"Ha, it's about my *favorite* gal again, Maggie," he said. We looked at him, waiting for what was coming next. "You know Nikos was late today, and Maggie was going berserk with his absence, right?" We nodded. Everyone had heard about Nikos' tardiness and Maggie walking everywhere looking for him. "So, listen to this. He showed up like… around 10ish, apologized for being late and told us he would review our project tonight if we could stay an hour later. OK, fine. Then, bitchy Maggie shows up like a crazy Harpy, screaming at Nikos."

Jane burst out laughing. "Are you serious? This is too funny to imagine. Maggie, the beautiful Harpy, a cruel, vicious female monster with a human face and the body of a bird cawing at the Greek hero."

"I'm telling you, my lovely, that woman is insanely jealous of the Greek."

"And what did he do?" I asked shyly, my stomach churned in disgust as I imagined Maggie coming onto Nikos as a vicious Harpy. She had no right to embarrass him publicly like that - who did she think she was? I felt sorry for Nikos.

"At first, he ignored her, but she kept yelling at him, asking where he had been all morning. He tried to calm her down and take her to his office but she didn't move until he answered her questions in front of all of us. It was really embarrassing," Curt told us. He ate some of his salad and took a sip of his iced tea before continuing. "So, he told her he had a last minute conference call with his museum director from Greece, and that it didn't concern her. He sounded furious with her scandalous behavior."

"Wow, she's really something else. Did she believe him?" Jane asked.

"She kept arguing with him, and asking why he didn't answer her calls and her texts. She even went to his place to see if he was OK, but there was no answer. And the security guard didn't let her drive inside the apartment complex. Oh, believe me. She was totally out of control. It amazed me how patient he was with her. I mean, I could tell he was furious but he didn't lose his cool."

"If he was on a conference call, he wasn't able to answer the phone or read his texts, I guess..." I mumbled, trying to validate Nikos' excuse.

"You're absolutely right, my queen," Curt said, "but the bitch was so blind she couldn't see that. Oh, well, I can't wait to see what will happen in the next chapter of their crazy relationship. Poor Nikos..." Jane smirked at me while Curt finished his salad. I knew what she was thinking: Maggie's behavior was not that of a business associate, far from it. And she was pushing Nikos to the limit. How much longer would he be able to endure Maggie's unpredictable demeanor?

Curt finished his meal and went back to the Antiquities department to work with Nikos. How I wished it was me! I didn't know when or where I would be in his arms again, but I hoped it would be soon. I was too anxious this morning because of our tardiness to think much about the future, so as soon as he dropped me off at Starbucks, I rushed to my car without saying much more than goodbye. When I started the engine, Nikos rolled down his window, waved at me and made a sign with his hand like he was going to call me later. And then he drove off.

When we finished eating, we walked out of Café Express into the restroom located next to the escalator. As I was applying lipstick, Maggie came in. She stopped as soon as she saw me, taken aback by my presence.

"Where were you this morning?" she asked insolently.

"Excuse me?" I asked, irritated by her audacity. Jane, who was washing her hands, stopped and stared at us.

"Where were you this morning?" Maggie asked again. "Why were you late?"

"That's none of your business," Jane chimed in. I knew she couldn't keep quiet.

"Stay out of it, Jane. I'm not talking to you," Maggie snapped at her.

"It's really none of your business, Maggie. Since when are you so interested in my whereabouts?" I asked. I saw Jane biting her lower lip in an attempt to be quiet and let me defend myself.

"Since you've been harassing my boyfriend, Sabrina. It's a strange coincidence that both of you were late today," she said.

"Don't you trust your boyfriend?" I teased her.

"I trust him, but I don't trust women like you, who come up with fake projects to get closer to him," Maggie responded, clenching her teeth. She was fuming. I wanted to smack her in the middle of her face, but instead, I took a deep breath.

"You're making a fool of yourself, and dragging your boyfriend with you into this madness. Haven't you noticed how ridiculous you've been acting because of him? It doesn't look good for a guest Professor to be involved in so much drama." Maggie gaped at me, astonished by my words. I don't think anyone had had the courage to bring her to her senses about her recent manners. Jane gave her a disdainful look. She turned around and left the restroom without saying anything else.

"That was great," Jane exclaimed. "You put the bitch in her place. Kudos for you!"

"I can't believe she had the nerve to confront me about me being late this morning. Really. This bitch can go to hell," I said.

"Well, let's see how her boyfriend will react," Jane annoyed me.

"He's not her boyfriend," I stated, as we left the restroom and walked back to our respective departments.

At the end of the day, I went home by myself, feeling lonely and missing Nikos. I hadn't seen him all day since morning, and I knew he was spending a few extra hours in the museum to recover the time he had missed. I longed to call him and see him again, but I didn't want to disturb him. He was probably as tired as I was from our amazing lovemaking the night before. It was better if I just went to bed and got some well needed rest, even though I was dying to find out how he was and how he felt after Maggie's public altercation in the museum. Lost in my thoughts, and longing for Nikos, I fell asleep.

When I got to the museum the next morning, all I wanted was to see Nikos. By mid morning, I hadn't heard from him yet, so I sent him a text. By lunch time, I hadn't received anything back from him and started to worry. I wondered if he was at the museum, or if he was so busy he hadn't had time to answer my

113

text. I was eager to see Curt during lunch to try to get the scoop about Nikos' whereabouts without asking around. I knew Curt would say something about Nikos or Maggie if I walked into him. But when Jane called to let me know her department was eating in - they had ordered pizza - she mentioned Curt and Robert had gone out to a restaurant on Montrose for lunch together. She hadn't seen Nikos and had no idea if he was in the museum. Obviously, she had to remind me Nikos' last name meant "unexplained" and it reflected what he was: mysterious. And possibly a liar, she added. I didn't want to worry too much about lack of news from him. After all, I knew how busy he was not only with his work at hand, but with all the other issues going on in Greece he had to deal with from a distance.

Later that afternoon, since I still hadn't heard from him, I sent him another text just telling him I missed him. After receiving no answer from him all day, I couldn't help but take a break and wander into the Antiquities department. I spotted Curt right away, playing docent to a couple of teenagers who were gathered around a Roman white marble panel. Tall, slender, with a white complexion and very curly blond hair, Curt looked happy and energized, like a skinny cherub, excitedly lecturing the teens about his favorite subject.

"This is a Roman white marble panel from the late 2nd century AD. Look at it carefully. It is a masterpiece of high-relief sculpture," Curt said. "It depicts a party of the god Dionysus, who, in Greek, is the god of wine, Bacchus. Can you identify which one is Dionysus?" he asked the attentive teens. They pointed to the smiley and happy chubby god surrounded by satyrs, and Curt nodded approvingly. "Is there anything else you want to know about it?" They shook their heads and moved on to look at another work of art. Curt saw me and hugged me cheerfully.

"Darling, what a surprise! You came to see me?" he asked.

I nodded. "I'm just taking a break and thought I'd visit my favorite department and my favorite friend."

"You're adorable," Curt said. "So, how is it going? Busy redesigning the African gallery?"

"Yes, sure, we're almost done. It's turning out beautiful. You have to come take a look before the grand opening of the gallery. What about here? How are you guys doing?" I was hoping he would say something about Nikos without me asking.

"Always a drama," Curt exclaimed. I looked at him with a curious expression, waiting for him to continue. "Our beloved friend Maggie has been under closed doors with her *boyfriend* all day long in his office," he said, pointing casually towards the door to Nikos' office. "They haven't come out once. Someone even brought them food during lunch. I wonder why she's keeping him locked in there, ha-ha-ha," Curt laughed maliciously. My heart almost stopped. Maggie and Nikos were locked in his office all day long? Was that the reason why he hadn't answered any of my texts? My insecurities popped up with full force when I thought about what Jane had said, and the way Maggie had confronted me again.

"Wow, never a dull moment in this department, right?" I tried to disguise my disappointment, when the door to Nikos' office all of a sudden burst open and both Nikos and Maggie emerged from inside the room, apparently ready to leave. They came to a stop upon seeing us, and Maggie's infuriated eyes rested on me. Nikos looked at me and Curt in surprise, bowed courteously, said a faint "good night" and walked out of the gallery, grabbing Maggie's arm so she would follow him. I gasped, unable to control my shock. What was going on? Curt turned to me.

"Yes, my sweetie, never a dull moment. And that Harpy hates you too. I could see the hatred in her eyes. What have you done to her, baby girl? Stay away from the Greek, it's proving to be dangerous," he said joking. But I was no longer in the mood to joke about it or laugh. I gave Curt a quick kiss on his cheek, and hurried out of the gallery.

As I rushed to the other side of the museum where my department was located, I tried to keep the tears from running. I walked into the restroom to compose myself, but I was too

115

upset to go back into the gallery, so I picked up my purse and left for the day. What was Nikos doing to me? 'I told you so,' I heard Jane's words echoing on my mind. No, it couldn't be. I refused to believe Nikos had been lying to me and that he was indeed dating Maggie. Not after yesterday, not after all he said to me, not after the way we made passionate love all night long. No, I refused to believe it. I was suffering, my heart was bleeding and I knew I had to talk to him to find out what was going on - why he had spent the whole day locked up in his office with Maggie and didn't answer my texts. A terrible thought crossed my mind and I imagined Nikos taking Maggie to his apartment and spending the night together. I wouldn't be able to handle it if I found out this was true.

Instead of going home, I drove to the mall. It was only about 4:45 pm and I didn't want to spend the rest of the evening wallowing in self pity, but I also didn't want to deal with Jane or any other company. I wanted to be alone, in a neutral zone, away from anything and anyone who reminded me of Nikos. The museum reminded me of Nikos, my apartment reminded me of Nikos, and even Starbucks reminded me of Nikos. At least, the mall was a place that wouldn't remind me of anything Greek, and where I would try to remove myself from the turmoil ravaging my heart. I left my cell phone in the car, so I didn't have to deal with any calls or texts. I spent the rest of the evening browsing the beautiful, elegant and colorful boutiques, and ended up not buying anything. But by the time I got home I was in a much better mood. I had entertained myself and was tired enough to go to bed right away and forget about the drama. And since the next day was a Saturday, I didn't have to set the alarm to wake me up early. So I took a shower, turned on Pandora on a classical music channel, and drifted off to sleep in Morpheus' arms, although he never offered me a dream that night.

****

Heavy knocks on the door awakened me. I looked drowsily at the clock by the bedside - it showed 9 am. Confused, I thought

116

I had forgotten to set the alarm, but then I realized it was Saturday. Who would be knocking on my door on Saturday morning if it was not early bird Jane? I looked for my cell phone to see if she had called, then I remembered I had left it in the car since last afternoon. The knocks persisted. I got up still half asleep, and walked to the living room wearing only my Victoria's Secret red lacy satin slip, thinking it was Jane for sure.

"Jane, I've told you not to wake me up early on the weekends," I said, opening the door abruptly.

"It's not Jane, it's me," the sexy voice of my Greek god resonated in my ears. I jumped back startled, now fully awake and aware I was dressed in skimpy and sexy lingerie. Nikos moved inside and closed the door behind him. "Do you always open the door dressed like this?" He looked at me with a smoldering glance. I stepped away from him, unsure what to say, taken aback by the vision of my Olympian god.

"I thought… it was Jane…" I stuttered.

"Well, it's not Jane. I'm here to check on you. You don't pick up your phone, and you don't answer my texts… so I had to come and see if you were OK."

I gaped at him. "*I* don't pick up my phone? *I* don't answer your texts? What are you talking about? *You* ignored me yesterday. And you were… you were locked all day with Maggie in your office and… I don't know what to think..." I said, trying to avoid his gaze. Nikos stared at me with hungry eyes.

"Do you want to cover yourself so we can talk, or do you want me to make love to you right here and right now?" he asked.

"What?" I gasped.

"It's better if you dress yourself. I'll wait here," he said calmly. I obeyed him and walked back to my bedroom, returning to the living room covered with the silk red robe that was a match to the slip underneath. Nikos was sitting on the sofa staring at me.

"OK, my goddess, this is better. For now," he stated. I blushed and sat on the chair opposite from him. "You didn't see my messages?"

"I left the phone in the car. I haven't checked it since last evening," I answered.

117

"I'm sorry I didn't answer you yesterday. I was caught up in a dinner with Mr. Wallendorf until late last night. After that, I called you to let you know what was happening but you didn't answer me last night or this morning."

"What was so important that you had to be with Maggie all day? Curt told me you didn't even get out of the office for lunch…"

"I told you I have business with the Wallendorfs, and I don't want Maggie harassing you. I don't like the way she goes around boasting about being my girlfriend and confronting you about it. You still don't believe me." Nikos' voice was serious but he appeared anxious, fidgeting with his car keys, which he was still holding.

"So why don't you tell her to stop it?"

"Maggie is a difficult person. She's used to getting everything she wants, and her father is willing to satisfy her every wish. But when it comes to me, I'm not her toy. Why can't you trust me?" Nikos said, still playing with his keys.

"She accosted me again, wanting to know why I was late that day. She thinks there's something going on between me and her *boyfriend*," I said almost sarcastically. Nikos threw his keys on the table and ran his fingers through his hair, in that sexy way he always did when he was exasperated or upset. He sighed.

"I'm sorry. This is getting more complicated than I thought."

"It's not your fault," I was quick to respond. "Maggie is out of control and she's known for being a jealous person. It's not the first time she's had fits because of a boyfriend."

"I'm not her boyfriend, so please stop referring to me like that." He sounded annoyed.

"I didn't mean to upset you. It's frustrating to know Maggie can't even see me without getting suspicious and jealous of you. What is really going on? Why is this getting more complicated than you thought? I really want to trust you."

"Mr. Wallendorf is getting more involved than he should and… the issue is that Greece's Ministry of Culture gave *carte blanche* for the museum to loan some pieces of the Gold Mycenaean Jewelry to a private collector who is a friend of Mr.

118

Wallendorf. There's a lot of money involved in this deal, of course, and truthfully, I have no idea how Mr. Wallendorf was able to break through the red tape of the museum's management," Nikos explained. He got up from the sofa and started to pace around the room, visibly restless.

"Why are you so worried about it?" I asked.

"I don't have a good feeling about it. Taking these jewels from the permanent collection is a risky business and involves a great deal of expertise. They're delicate, fragile, and extremely valuable. And Mr. Wallendorf put Maggie in charge of it. She is driving me crazy." He stopped pacing and stared deeply at me. "I need to take a break away from it… Do you want to go somewhere for the weekend?" he blurted out.

"For the weekend?" I asked, astonished by his unexpected suggestion.

"Yes. Let's go to San Antonio. Today. I'd love to see the Spanish Missions built in the 18th century. And I want to spend the weekend with you." Nikos caught me by surprise once again. Oh, my Greek god, of course I want to spend the weekend with you. I want to spend my whole life with you. You make me feel so complete when I'm with you and being away from here will be a refreshing break for both of us. He came closer to where I was sitting, and squatted down in front of me so he could look into my eyes.

"Do you want to spend the weekend with me in San Antonio?" he whispered with his mouth so close to my face I could feel his fresh breath. I nodded eagerly. His mouth descended upon mine and we embraced in an ardent kiss. My skin tingled, anticipating his next movement. But he let go of the steady pressure of his mouth on mine and released me. I stared at him, breathless, with my mouth still half open, not ready to let him go. "Get dressed, my goddess, let's get going," he said.

"Now?" I asked, frustrated that he had stopped kissing me and was urging me to go.

"Yes. I want you more than you can imagine," he said, "and I'll have the whole weekend in San Antonio to love you." I blushed, and giving him a girlish smile, I jumped out of the love seat and rushed to my bedroom to prepare myself for a weekend adventure with my Greek hero. I packed a few dresses just in case, t-shirts, sandals and Victoria's Secret lingerie in a duffel bag, making sure not to forget my bottle of *Chance* perfume, and took a quick shower while Nikos was waiting for me. When I came out of the bedroom, I was wearing a pink V-neck t-shirt, a pair of Michael Kors jeans and flat sandals. Nikos got up from the sofa and gave me an approving look. He took the duffel bag from my hand and we left the apartment.

Before we got into the Jeep Cherokee he had rented a couple of days ago, I picked up my cell phone which was left in the car the whole night. Among the messages I hadn't answered, there were Nikos' texts and missed calls from last night and earlier this morning, as well as a text from Jane, inviting me to go to Curt and Robert's in the afternoon for a pool party. I sent her a quick text to let her know I was going on a road trip and would get back to her Sunday evening. Oh, how I wished I could see Jane's face when she read my text, dying of curiosity the whole weekend to find out about my escapade.

Nikos got inside the car and turned on the music. A powerful, melancholy ballad echoed from the speakers. Linkin Park's Waiting for the End was playing and the words reflected the inevitable. It was almost as if we were being given signs about our impending separation, about the awful reality of waiting for the end, which was out of our control and so hard to let go.

Nikos was silent for a minute, listening intently to Chester Bennington's words. "Do you like this song?" he asked me.

"Yes, I do," I answered. "This is one of my favorite bands… don't you like it?"

"I do, actually. But I was thinking what a coincidence that it started playing right now. It's such a sad song, isn't it?"

"Yes, it is…" I said, looking into his eyes. "Waiting for the end… it is sad and heartbreaking... knowing that what's coming is the end…"

He stared at me, paying attention to the lyrics. The beautiful, sad song implied that their love relationship was never meant

120

to last anyways, and although the singer wished it was different, he was trying to forget whatever had happened in their past. I could and would never be able to forget what had happened between us.

"What are you thinking about?" I asked.

"We both know the day when I have to leave is approaching soon," he said, kissing my hand and giving me his faint smile.

I breathed deeply. "It's hard to think about it," I said, "but I want to be with you while you're here." He looked at me with his hypnotizing eyes and started the car. I couldn't believe I was going to San Antonio with the man of my dreams. But now the heartbreaking lyrics were on my mind, reminding me of the inevitable day he would leave.

When we got to his place, I waited in the car while he went in to pack. He was back in no time with a glowing expression, looking almost like a happy child who had just received a much expected gift. I looked at him with a smile on my face. I wished I could release his tension and make him happy forever. Nikos was everything I had always wanted, and I was overjoyed to be able to spend a weekend with him, carefree and without the weight of work, or Maggie's irritating presence threatening our relationship. We needed this time to get to know each other better, even though, in the back of my mind, the ghost of the separation lingered, the annoying knowledge that soon Nikos was going back to Greece and I didn't know when or if I would ever see him again. But for now, he was mine.

Chapter 16

We had a relaxed and cheerful drive to San Antonio, chatting while listening to music. Nikos wanted to know more about me.

"My parents live in Miami," I told him, "they love the beach and found a great retirement community over there. I usually visit them during the summer when I'm on vacation, but this year I'm doing the internship. What about your parents? You told me your mother was a ballerina, right? What about your dad?"

"I haven't heard from my father in several years."

"What happened?"

"My mother was a ballerina, as you know, and my father was a musician. He fell in love with one of the Russian ballerinas who used to come and perform with my mother's ballet company. One day he just ran away with her to Paris. He... abandoned us."

"Oh... I'm so sorry to hear this. It must have been very hard on you... and your mother..."

"My mother is a very strong woman. She raised me and my brother by herself, and it was not easy. I have to make sure she will always be taken care of. I'd never forgive myself if something happened to her."

"I didn't know you had a brother. What does he do?" I was curious. Nikos hadn't talked much about his family, although he once mentioned family issues after one of the phone calls he received.

"Yes, I have a brother. He's younger, and... well, he keeps my mother busy and I'm worried about her. But enough about my family. Tell me more about you. So you broke up with your boyfriend a few months ago?" He changed the subject brusquely, and I could tell he didn't want to talk much about his family.

"Yes, unfortunately we had very different interests and it didn't work out. What about you?" I asked. He shook his head and smiled at me.

"With all the work, studying, projects... it's almost impossible to maintain a healthy relationship with someone. I don't go out that often. My last girlfriend couldn't handle my archaeological explorations. I was gone too much. It just didn't work." Oh, I can handle your archaeological explorations, I thought to myself. "And that's why I wanted to apologize to you when I told you I didn't want to hurt you and I shouldn't have touched you," he continued.

"What does it have to do with it?"

"My father left my mother and I know so well how much it hurt her, how the rejection and abandonment made her feel. I'd hate myself if I instilled so much pain in a human being like that. It's not worth it. I have to be more careful and control myself better. I made a mistake when I slept with Maggie, but it's not the same with you. It really bothers me because I don't want to hurt you and I know I have to leave."

"But... you can't run away from relationships all the time, Nikos. Don't you need to feel... close to someone?"

"It's hard to get attached to a person when I know how much damage abandonment can cause. And I'm worried about you."

"It's not the same," I said. I wanted to hug him and kiss him and hold him in my arms. "You're not... abandoning me. I'm well aware you have to go back to Greece and... I hate thinking about it, but I allowed you into my life and I have to accept the risks. I don't regret it. I wanted you."

He reached for my hand and held it tight, but didn't say anything else. It was lunch time when we arrived in San Antonio. Nikos had made a surprise reservation for a suite at the Hotel Mokara from his phone, and he didn't tell me until we got there. Our luxurious suite was almost as large as my apartment, with a gorgeous living area, a spacious bath, and a magnificent view of the River Walk from a private balcony. If his intentions were to impress me, he had accomplished them.

"This is beautiful," I exclaimed, opening the door to the balcony to appreciate the festive view of one of the city's main attractions. "You shouldn't have..." I murmured. Nikos came

123

to the balcony behind me and put his arms around my waist, giving me a lingering kiss on the nape of my neck.

"I wanted the best room for my goddess," he whispered with his sensual and husky voice. My heart skipped a beat and I felt dizzy with desire. You have no idea what you do to me, my Odysseus, I want you so much and I will wait for you forever like Penelope, I thought. I was shaking, as Nikos continued to kiss and lightly peck my neck and earlobe. I sighed, completely heated up by his touches, and turned around to face him, eager to kiss him and get my desire satisfied. But instead of kissing my mouth, he held my hands and brought them up to his mouth, kissing them both with his soft, moist lips.

"It's lunchtime. Let's go down and find a place to eat," he said, letting go of me. I looked at him like a hungry lioness, although I was not hungry for food, and he knew it.

"Be patient, my goddess," he whispered, smirking lightly, completely aware of my arousal and with an apparent intention of teasing me to my limits.

"Why are you doing this?" I asked, unable to disguise my frustration.

"Because I love to see what I do to you. I love to see your reaction when I touch you. And because I want you to desire me as much as I desire you." His eyes looked like two incandescent balls of fire and I could almost feel them burning my own.

"But I do," I pleaded. "I desire you more than you know."

"I want you, Sabrina. And I want us to go out and have something to eat and enjoy ourselves. I want to build our desire for tonight," Nikos said. I could barely contain myself thinking about what would be in store for me tonight, living my Greek dream.

We left the suite and took the elevator to the lobby. Nikos held my hand and we strolled by the River Walk looking for a restaurant. We settled for a Tex-Mex place that boasted to have the best margaritas in town. Nikos ordered the food, and we sat next to each other looking like two teenagers in love, while we sipped our margaritas and watched people walking by. Boats floated in the river, full of excited tourists listening with interest to their tour guides and waving at the people who stood watching them over the bridges. It was such a pleasurable afternoon and it felt even better because we didn't have to worry about time or space. We were just enjoying each other's company, in the comfort of knowing no one would interrupt our loving weekend.

After lunch and two margaritas, I felt completely relaxed and somewhat tipsy. Nikos held me by the hand and we walked around, while I laughed and giggled like I was in my honeymoon with the man of my dreams. I knew Nikos was amused by my behavior, so content and stress-free, taking in every minute of a momentary joy I wished would never vanish. Why would we have to go back to reality in a few days? No, I thought to myself, I won't let these heavy and dark clouds rain on my sunny spot. Right then and there, I was the happiest woman on the planet. We had so much fun that afternoon. We took a boat tour, visited the Alamo and then went up to the observation deck of the Tower of the Americas to look at the city from above.

"How do you like it?" I asked, while holding hands with him. We stood by the panoramic window enjoying the view.

"I'm so glad we came here." He turned to me and wrapped his arms around my waist, pulling me closer to him and giving me a quick kiss on the forehead. "I can't wait to be with you tonight," he said almost in a whisper. My body trembled with expectation; I also couldn't wait to be with him. Here, now, everywhere, forever.

"We will have some wine at the Charter House Restaurant and after that, we will go to the hotel. How does it sound?" he asked, still holding me in his arms. Somehow he had everything already planned.

"It sounds good. I can't wait," I said. Nikos took my hand again and walked me to the restaurant's bar. Happy hour was going on, and we sat facing the huge windows overlooking the city. He ordered two glasses of white wine and we enjoyed the drink in silence, taking in the peace surrounding us. What a blissful moment. I knew I would cherish these moments with Nikos forever, so I took my phone out of my purse.

"Can we take a picture together?" I asked him.

"Sure," Nikos said, and holding my phone at arm's length, he snapped a picture of us, capturing our smiles as a testimony of the passion shining through our eyes.

By the time we got to the hotel, I wanted to take a shower, refresh myself and get ready for the night ahead, and I needed time to prepare my lingerie and beauty routine. Nikos turned on the satellite radio in the huge room and sat down to check his emails and texts while I walked to the spacious bathroom under the sound of Imagine Dragons.

On top of the vanity, Nikos had placed his toiletries. I found a bottle of his cologne next to his shaving cream, toothpaste and toothbrush. It was Dolce & Gabbana Light Blue, Nikos' scent that drove me crazy. I sprayed it on my hand and smelled it. Yes, it was Nikos' signature smell and I really loved it. I wished I could bathe in him forever.

When I left the clean and spacious bathroom, wrapped in the velvety cotton towel, Nikos had already removed his clothes and stood like a marble statue staring out the window. I gasped when I saw his magnificent body and he turned around, walking in my direction as soon as he realized I was in the room.

"Do I scare you?" he said, getting closer to me. I couldn't help noticing he was as hard and big as I'd ever seen before.

"N-no," I stuttered. It was difficult to breathe when he was this close to me. And with no clothes. He lifted my chin with his fingers to get a closer look at my face and all of a sudden, he gripped me by the waist and lowered his head to open his mouth on mine. He kissed me hard, with an almost violent passion, while I wrapped my arms around his broad shoulders, letting my towel fall on the floor. Just as unexpectedly as he had grabbed me, he released me, making me wobble in search of balance for a second.

126

"I'll be right back," he said, "I think you're ready for me." He went into the bathroom and turned on the shower. I was dizzy with pleasure and expectation. I dried myself quickly and slathered lotion on my arms, chest, legs and feet, dabbed a few drops of *Chance* behind my ears, on the back of my pulses and in my cleavage area, then brushed my hair and got dressed. I wore my Victoria's Secret silky satin lace black slip, no panties, and threw in the matching silky black robe on top, wrapping the silk belt around my waist. I was ready for Nikos, and when he came out of the shower with the towel wrapped around his waist, I walked towards him and threw my arms around his neck.

"Are you all mine now?" I asked eager to finally be in his arms.

"Yes, my goddess, I'm all yours now," he said, and enveloped me with his strong and well defined arms. I reached for his lips and tasted him with my tongue, opening my mouth to explore his. He returned my kiss with intensity and passion, and lifted me off of the floor, carrying me passionately to the amazingly comfortable king size bed of the hotel room. He laid me down on the feathers filled duvet, which made me feel like I was on top of a cloud. Yes, I was on top of the world, floating among the clouds on Mount Olympus with my seductive god. He pulled the towel from his waist and let it fall on the carpeted floor, revealing once again his magnificence. I stared at him in anticipation. He climbed on the bed next to me and slowly untied the knot of the silk belt wrapped around my waist, and opened the robe to find me dressed in the sexy black slip. He removed the robe from me and lifted both my arms above my head. With a quick movement, he wrapped the silk belt he had just untied around my wrists, immobilizing my arms. My heart beat faster.

"What are you doing?" My voice was shaky to almost a whisper. He kissed my lips softly and stroked my hair with a gentle motion.

"Shhhhh…" he whispered next to my ear, breathing on my neck. "Trust me, my goddess, just trust me and relax. I'm not going to hurt you. All I want is to please you and love you," and his mouth was on mine again, invading me sensually. Out

127

of nowhere he produced a sleeping mask and wrapped it around my eyes, blindfolding me. I protested.

"I want to see you." I was nervous and he was frightening me. I had no idea of his intentions.

"You will see me later, now I want you to just feel me. Just feel what I will do to you. Can you trust me?" he asked me. I let out a loud sigh. How could I not trust him? I wanted him desperately since the morning when he had come over to my apartment and kissed me before we drove to San Antonio. The tension had been building and his teasing had not stopped all day. I was absolutely crazy for this man, and whatever he wanted to do to me, I knew I wouldn't be able to say no. My heart was pounding violently through the thin layer of my silk slip. Everything was dark and I couldn't move, and Nikos was on top of me kissing my mouth with furious passion while I squirmed under his masculine body trying to accommodate him in between my legs.

"No, not yet, my goddess," he said, taking his weight off me and moving to my side. I moaned, unable to say anything. The sensation was strange, yet I loved being held captive by him, unable to move my arms and unable to see him. He got off the bed and I had no idea what he was doing or where he went, but it didn't take long for me to feel him climbing back on the bed again. His hands moved lightly under my silk slip and with a quick motion, he removed it, pulling it over my head. I was completely naked under his gaze and although I couldn't see his face, I heard his heavy breathing. It was nerve-wracking not to see him.

Without warning, I felt something icy cold right on my lips and shivered, realizing it was an ice cube. Nikos slid the ice cube down my chin slowly, moving it down my neck and chest till he reached my breasts. He moved the ice cube in a circular motion around my right breast and slowly up to my nipple, while my skin tingled in excitement. I was getting very cold and I knew my skin was covered in goose bumps. What an exquisite feeling… He moved the ice cube to my left breast and repeated what he had done on the other, while I felt his wet and warm tongue on my right nipple, sucking it gently and warming it with his hot breath. My body squirmed with pleasure, and my back arched, lifting my nipple closer to his mouth. His pressure was firm, and without taking his mouth off me, he moved the ice cube from my other nipple and slid it down my belly, rubbing it gently around my navel. I let out a faint cry. I'd never felt my nipples hardening this much before.

Nikos alternated his mouth between my nipples, sucking and biting them gently, warming them with his hot, sweet breath, while he moved the icy cube down my navel, making me consciously aware of my arousal. I moaned and sighed with the indescribable sensation overwhelming my senses. He stopped suddenly and the next minute he was on top of me again, holding my arms firmly while his mouth came hungrily at mine. He kissed me ardently, and his tongue dove inside to explore every corner of my mouth, leaving me once again breathless. After the cold and hot sensory stimulation, his mouth left mine and started going down my body. He repeated the motions of his wet tongue on my nipples, and licked my body as if I was covered in chocolate.

"You smell delicious," he whispered, "I love *Chance*." I let out a small cry again, my insides burning with such excitement I could hardly contain myself. His fingers stroked my skin lightly like a feather going throughout my body, making me shudder from his delicate touch. His lips brushed against my skin, kissing me so softly they almost tickled, and all of a sudden he lifted my legs up, exposing me completely to him. I was quivering, I wanted to see him and touch him, but blindfolded with my arms tied up over my head, I was completely under his submission.

His lips continued to explore my skin, touching me where I was most vulnerable and sensitive. I moaned louder, almost unable to contain my anticipation. His fingers had a strong grip on my legs but my hips swayed in harmony with his tongue's skillful moves, maintaining the pressure and the pace, licking me, kissing me and tasting me. Unable to resist the urge any longer, I let out a loud moan, and as he realized I was about to climax, he climbed on top and entered me. We rocked back and forth under my pulsating release, until it culminated with his own pleasure. Nikos let out a quiet moan and moved away from me to untie the silky knot wrapped around my wrists. My arms were sore from the stillness, but I didn't care. I removed the sleeping mask from my eyes, trying to re-adapt them to the light, looking for Nikos. He was lying by my side, with his smoldering eyes wide open watching me with a grin on his face.

"Welcome to the light, my goddess," he greeted me, touching my hair with tenderness. I smiled at him and snuggled closer, resting my head on his shoulder.

"You are incredible," I said. He kissed my forehead and wrapped me in his arms. We lay curled up together in bed, resting our naked and satisfied bodies after our passionate lovemaking until we fell asleep.

When I woke up Nikos was not in bed. I scrunched my eyes up in the darkness to see the clock. It was still very early in the morning. The room was silent, except for the faint sound of the satellite radio still playing. Lifehouse's Broken was on - yet another song that reminded me of the inevitable, making me shudder just to think I would lose Nikos. I had to hold on to him as much as I could. Every word of the song made me cringe. I knew the pain would be unbearable and I would, for sure, fall apart with a broken heart. I couldn't even think about being away from him. Why did these sad songs kept playing all the time to remind me of our impending separation? And where was Nikos? I called out his name almost in panic.

"I'm right here," I heard him from the adjacent living room area of our huge suite. "Would you like me to bring you a glass of water?"

He walked back into the room before I could answer, holding two glasses of cold water. I could barely make up his silhouette against the dark room. He turned on a small lamp by his side of the bed and handed me one of the glasses.

"Thanks," I said, holding the cup and drinking the cool, refreshing water.

"What's wrong?" he asked. I noticed he was paying attention to the song still playing on the background.

"I thought you had left... I mean, I probably had a dream, I don't know. What were you doing?"

"I'm not leaving you. Don't pay attention to every song's sad lyrics," Nikos said, shaking his head. "I was checking my email for messages from home." He finished drinking his water and placed the empty glass on the table, then climbed back onto the bed and buried his head on my neck, breathing deeply and resting his hand on my waistline.

"How is everything going?"

"Issues with my brother. My mother is worried. But I'll call her later. Right now I just want to be here with you," he said, kissing my neck.

"I love your smell, I love your taste, I love everything about you," I said, wrapping my arms around his torso, getting closer to him. "I'm completely in love with you, and I have no idea what I'm going to do when you leave."

"Don't think about it for now," he whispered, moving his hands from my belly to my thigh and tickling me with his fingers, using slow, circular movements. I felt the heat turn up in between my legs and pressed them against his. His hand moved down and he inserted a finger inside of me to feel my moisture. "You're ready

for me again, my goddess," he said, growing in anticipation.

"I'm always ready for you," I answered and kissed him passionately, mounting on him.

****

After we wasted ourselves on each other once more, immersed in an irresistible desire, Nikos got out of bed, opened the curtains of the panoramic window and then got into the shower. I moved lazily, not wanting to believe it was already Sunday and the next day everything was going to be back to normal again, and this reality would be but a dream etched forever on my mind. I can't get depressed right now, I thought.

131

We still have all day ahead of us and Nikos wants to go sightseeing in the San Antonio Missions National Historical Park. I had to disguise my apprehension, which was growing just to think about him leaving the country. Nikos didn't want to talk about it, and during this dreamy weekend we never really discussed our relationship in a deeper level. All I knew was that I was completely in love with this man and being apart from him was an inconceivable thought.

We went downstairs for breakfast at Ostra, the hotel's romantic riverfront restaurant. Nikos was animated with our plans for the day. He had collected brochures from the hotel's concierge and was studying the route and history of the Spanish Missions of Old San Antonio. Although I had been to the missions years ago, visiting them with Nikos would be an unforgettable experience. How I wish this weekend would never end.

The waiter brought the mimosas Nikos had ordered. "Thank you for a perfect weekend," he said, lifting the tall champagne flute to me.

"Cheers," I responded, "and hoping for an unforgettable afternoon." I moved my champagne flute next to his and they touched lightly. "I wished this weekend would never end," I muttered, taking a sip of my mimosa.

"Enjoy it, my beautiful goddess," Nikos said, reaching out for my hand.

"I can't stop thinking you will be gone soon, and I will be devastated," I said.

"I want you to enjoy the day with me and be present in the now, in this moment. I don't want you to think about the future, we don't know what it holds. Just think about now," he said, tightening his grip on my hand.

"What's going to happen when you go? Will I ever see you again?" I couldn't help it any longer.

"Of course you will see me again. I'd love to show you Greece," he said.

"I'd love that…" I said, dreaming about seeing the Acropolis with him.

"But now, just enjoy the day. We will worry about tomorrow later."

I looked at him. "I'll try. All I want is for this day to last forever."

After we finished our breakfast, we checked out of the hotel and drove towards Mission Concepcion. Nikos parked the car and we explored the beautiful mission grounds, which held the best preserved church of the trail, founded in 1731. It was refreshing to see Nikos the archaeologist in action. He was so detailed in his exploration, explaining to me several facts about the site which I would not have noticed, if it wasn't for the eyes of an expert in ruins. The site was so well preserved we could still see original interior paintings at the walls and ceilings of the building.

Next, we drove to what was called the *Queen of the Missions*. Mission San Jose was the best known of the Texas missions. It used to be a major social center, encircled by massive stone walls for defense in a beautiful compound. Unfortunately some of the structures were in ruins, but Nikos loved to see the partially reconstructed frescoes, which were still visible at the base of the bell tower, and the famous Rose Window, considered one of the finest examples of baroque architecture in North America.

"The archeology in this country is so recent," he mentioned, while appreciating and taking photos of the structure.

"Not even close to the age of your findings," I said. "I didn't think you'd be so impressed with it. You're so used to objects and places found many centuries ago, not just 200 years ago…"

"Never underestimate the passion of an archaeologist," he said, smiling at me. "Everything that brings to surface our history and tries to explain or make us understand why and how the development of humanity happens is impressive. Look at this window." He paused, came close to me and wrapped his hands around my waist. "You can see a high skill of craftsmanship from the 1700's, when it was built. It was beautifully sculptured in the stone." I laid my head on his shoulder and breathed his sensual scent.

"Yes, Dr. Nikos Soulis, you're an expert," I said, turning to kiss him. He kissed me back with his hot, luscious lips and I could sense his arousal.

"Thank you," he said upon releasing me from his kiss. "I couldn't have asked for a better company to explore these sites."

I looked deep into his eyes. "I love what you do and I'll always support you, Nikos. All I want is to trust you and be by your side. I don't care if I get hurt. This is the best weekend of my life and I'm the one who needs to thank you for giving me a chance to get to know you better."

He stared at me, gave me his seductive, faint smile and holding my hand, he led me out to the car.

The four mission sites, linked by a road, were easy to drive to, and they were well preserved and still in use as active churches. Our last stop before heading back to Houston was Mission San Francisco de la Espada with its unusual door and stone entrance archway. After Nikos took several pictures of the beautiful architectural façade, we got back in the car to return home.

I was hot, exhausted, and visibly saddened with the end of our adventure. Nikos stopped at a gas station to fill up the tank and bought a few bottles of cold water and snacks. We had a nice drive back and most of the time we chatted about the missions and our good time in San Antonio. Nikos sounded and acted much more relaxed than I had ever seen him, as if nothing else mattered but us and our sensual weekend getaway. I sensed he purposely avoided talking about the end of the summer and his impending return. I won't talk about it and spoil the end of this unforgettable weekend, I thought to myself. Nikos still had roughly three weeks to spend in Houston and I was hoping we would have plenty of time to talk about it, although I couldn't see a happy outcome with him being so far away. But our love was magical, and I wanted to hold on to the fairy tale, hoping my Greek god would be mine forever.

"I'll bring your bag upstairs for you," Nikos said when he parked in front of my apartment. I opened the door and he walked in, placing my duffel bag on the floor. I turned to him in apprehension. I wanted him again, I wanted him to spend the night with me and love me like he did the night before. I couldn't stop desiring this man. "I better get going," he said, combing his hair with his fingers as he usually did when he was upset or anxious. "It's getting late, we have to go back to reality tomorrow and I have to check my messages again. I will be busy tonight with calls from Greece."

I wrapped my hands around his waist, bringing him closer to me. "Can you spend the night here with me?"

"I'd love to, but I'm afraid I'll have too much work to do tonight."

"Can I see you at the museum tomorrow, then?" I asked.

"Of course. What about we meet at the sculpture garden around 10 am for a break? I'll see you tomorrow. You need to rest too, my goddess," he said, lowering his head to kiss me. I opened my mouth in loving abandon, allowing his tongue to invade me and taste me passionately.

In the blink of an eye, my Greek hero was gone, and I was left alone in my apartment, longing to be with him again. Maggie's face resurfaced in my thoughts, like a ghost creeping up on my mind, reminding me she was a deceitful presence, claiming Nikos as hers, and imprisoning him under her claws, like the Harpy Jane had described. I just hoped I wouldn't see her any time soon, because if I did, I would have a very hard time controlling my jealousy, especially after the incredible weekend I had just spent with Nikos. I need to come down from Olympus, I thought, and be ready to enter Tartarus tomorrow...

Before going to bed, I checked my messages and emails. I had put my phone aside and hadn't checked anything since San Antonio. There were several messages, especially from Jane, who was dying to find out what had happened to me.

"What road trip was that?" she immediately jumped into the issue as soon as she answered her phone.

"Hello, my friend, how are you? How was your weekend?" She noticed my sarcasm.

"I'm sorry, Sabrina dear. But you drive me crazy with curiosity!"

I laughed. "I knew you'd be crazy to find out where I was. Are you ready for the truth?" I teased.

"It smells like Greek to me," Jane hinted. I laughed again. "You seem to be in a hell of a good mood, laughing so much," she said. "Go ahead, tell me about it, you crazy woman. Did you prepare your will? Because, you know, Maggie will probably hire a hit man."

"He's not dating Maggie, Jane, and I believe him. If he was, do you think he would be able to get rid of her for the whole weekend to go to San Antonio with me?"

"Wow, you guys went to San Antonio? What a nice getaway. Well, he may be convincing to you, but I still have my suspicions. Who knows what kind of lies he might tell Maggie to get her off his back for the weekend? But since you sound so happy… I am to assume Greek god was amazing…"

"He was more than amazing. It was the best weekend of my life and I have no idea what I'm going to do when he leaves. I'm so in love with him, you won't believe…"

"Oh, my dear, yes, I believe. I can totally hear you. You're so wrapped around his finger… he's that good, huh? And what does he say about his departure and your, er… affair?"

"He is that good, yes, better than that. But he didn't say anything about his leaving. He sort of avoided it the whole weekend. Every time I tried to talk about it, he changed subjects or told me to enjoy the moment with him and not think about the future. I'm so scared. I don't want to lose him, ever."

"You know it's inevitable; he will have to go back to Greece. The problem is you're too serious about him, and it seems what Greek god wanted was to have a great passionate weekend with a nice girl like you. I'm sorry to tell you that, but you need to wake up to reality, Sabrina dear."

"No, that's not it…" I mumbled. Somehow Jane's words made a lot of sense but I was in denial. I couldn't believe Nikos regarded me just as a temporary fling. He said he wanted to know me better if we had more time, and he'd love to show me Greece. And he told me the story of his father abandoning his mother, something he didn't want to do to someone else. He didn't want to hurt me. I had to hold on to the hope we were in a relationship that was going to last more than a few weeks. But then, I was creating my own illusion. I knew how hard it was to maintain a long distance relationship – and it was not just Houston and San Antonio. It was Houston and Athens. 6,322 miles of Atlantic Ocean and Europe would soon be between us.

"I know you just spent a wonderful weekend with him but please, come down to earth soon. Regardless of what kind of relationship he has with Maggie, whether it is business or a past romance, or a lie, she is real and lives here. I'd hate for her to become your number one enemy. She could make your life miserable. And Nikos… well, he will be history soon. Just keep the memories." What Jane said was cruel, raw and real.

I sighed. "Great way to end a fabulous fairy tale weekend."

"I'm sorry. I didn't mean to make you upset, but I hate to see where this is taking you. Which is, literally nowhere. And you deserve better, my friend, don't break your heart."

Through my window, I watched the sun going down, finally ending a long summer day. I knew I would have a long night thinking about my bleak future with Nikos. I needed music to soothe me, and as soon as I turned on the radio, Three Doors Down's Here Without You was playing. I recalled Nikos telling me not to pay attention to sad songs. But what could I do if every time music was playing, the lyrics talked about separation and heartbreak? Coincidentally or not, I took it as a sign, a premonition maybe, reminding me of what I had been conscious of all along, from the very first time I laid my eyes upon Nikos. And I heard myself singing the words, like an oracle, forecasting my loneliness and yearning for him. I was there without him and he would always be in my dreams.

And so I drifted off to sleep, painfully aware the next few weeks in the museum would likely be the most heartbreaking ones of my life.

Chapter 17

The more I thought about my feelings for Nikos and considered everything that was happening, the more confused I got. The only thing I knew for sure is I loved to be in his arms. I felt safe, secure and protected when I was with him – but that was the problem: when I was with him. When I was not with him, all these feelings vanished, and insecurity dominated every cell of my body. Much about Nikos was still unknown, unfamiliar, evasive, and there was no time to get to know him better. I had to trust my instincts. Unfortunately, they were telling me to flee. It was a matter of time before desolation took over. I knew the risks associated with becoming involved with a person from out of town and I had insisted in taking those risks, because I couldn't resist Nikos. Jane had been blunt enough to wake me up, and although I hated it, she might be right. I wanted to trust Nikos, but there was no guarantee he was telling me the truth. Nikos was as mysterious as his last name suggested.

I was meeting him at 10 am in the Cullen Sculpture Garden, just across the street from the museum, and I was looking forward to seeing him and finding out what was happening on his side of the world. There were a couple of visitors browsing the garden and contemplating the beautiful sculptures. An art student sat in front of Rodin's bronze statue, The Walking Man, making sketches. I found Nikos waiting for me at one of the park benches, holding two Starbucks cups.

"This is your favorite, isn't it? I told Rodney it was for you," he said, extending his hand to offer me a cup of mocha Frappuccino. He gave me his sexy smile and I had to resist the temptation of kissing him right there.

"Yes, thanks. That's so thoughtful of you! You had time to run to Starbucks and get coffee from my favorite barista?"

"I know you like it, so I stopped over there to get these before heading here. I'm just arriving for the day," he said.

"Isn't Maggie going to be looking for you all over the place?" I asked, a little worried.

"No. She is aware I'm coming late. I was on the phone with her father most of the morning. And it's Monday, she's not volunteering today. Don't worry about Maggie."

"Is everything else OK?"

"The transfer of the Gold Mycenaean Jewelry pieces to Mr. Wallendorf's European friend's collection is happening tomorrow morning in Greece, which should be around 2 am our time. I'm still concerned about it. To tell you the truth, I'm against this loan. I wish I was there to either stop it or oversee it."

"I hope everything goes well. Did you have a good night?"

"If being on the phone most of the night can be called a good night," he scoffed. "What about you? Did you rest enough, my sexy goddess?"

I blushed at his question, thinking about the wonderful weekend we had just spent. "Yes, I rested, but I'd rather have spent it with you."

He grinned. "Don't get me too excited or I'll make love to you right here in the garden."

Oh, my Olympian, how can you tease me like that? I could feel my nipples getting harder just thinking about being touched by him. I sucked on the straw and gulped the cold Frappuccino to cool off. Once I was in his presence, there was nothing I could do but succumb to his seduction. Any reasoning left in me was gone, and I stood paralyzed, ready for him to do with me as he pleased. He was staring at me with hungry eyes, always relentlessly studying my reactions to his words and gestures.

"Do... do you want to come over to my place later today?" I asked.

"I'd love to. But the transfer is happening in the middle of the night and I have to stay put. I won't be able to rest until I know these jewels are safely locked in Mr. Wallendorf's friend's private collection in England."

I shook my head, disappointed. Time was running fast, he would be gone soon, and I wanted the impossible. As usual, Nikos seemed to be reading my mind.

"Don't be upset." He reached for my hand, held it up and lifted it to his lips, sliding the tip of his tongue slowly over the inside of my wrist. I closed my eyes and shivered, as the sensation sent a shot of sexual tension right in between my legs. With a subtle movement, he inserted my index finger inside his hot, humid mouth and sucked on it with a gentle pressure. I let out a gasp and opened my eyes, staring at him in astonishment. His dark expressive eyes were on me the whole time, studying my reaction. He let go of my hand, and I was sure he knew I was a pool of moisture, ready for him.

"I'm sorry, I couldn't resist you," he said. "I want you. As soon as this deal is over, I'll come to you. Hopefully tomorrow night." I gulped. I could hardly say anything. My heart was pounding. Nikos was so much more than I could ever have hoped for and he knew exactly what to do to drive me crazy. Eros. "Come on, my beautiful goddess, let's go to work," he said.

We walked quietly to the museum trying to appease the strong sexual tension between us. I had to wait another night before my Olympian god would take me again. How could I survive without him?

To my surprise, Jane, Robert and Curt were sitting by the main entrance in an animated chat when we walked in. There was no way for us to split and pretend we hadn't walked in together. Jane looked at me with a naughty expression.

"Dr. Soulis. How nice to see you! I thought you were not coming in today," Curt exclaimed upon seeing us. Nikos walked up to them and I followed him.

"Good morning, everyone. Nice seeing you too. I'm here for half the day today. Things in Greece are keeping me busy and awake at night more than I wanted to," he said.

Curt looked at me with a smirk. I was sure if he had had any doubts about my involvement with Nikos, our showing up together now had just confirmed it.

"Why don't they leave you alone if they know you're working here in a totally different time zone?" Jane asked. I knew she was trying to catch Nikos in some kind of lie.

"It doesn't matter, I'm responsible for the department. It's not like I'm on vacation. I need to be aware of everything - it's part of the job," Nikos said in a very professional tone. He was so composed and usually had great answers for any questions that might sound compromising, and it was interesting to see how he never lost his cool, not even with Maggie. I was just thankful she wasn't at the museum today.

"I'll see you guys later," Nikos said, bowing towards us.

"Are you going to our department? I'm coming with you," Curt said, waving us goodbye and following Nikos.

"Take a seat here," Jane said as they left, pointing to the chair Curt had just vacated.

"My break is over, I need to go back to work," I said.

"Just stay here for five more minutes," Robert insisted. I sat down. "Maggie is going to kill you, girl," he said.

"Robert. It's not what you're thinking. I… you know I'm working on a project and…"

He interrupted me. "Cut it out, love. I can see the sparkle in your eyes when you're in his presence. Your secret is safe with me, cross my heart," he said. "But you need to be a little less obvious when Maggie is around. He's her boyfriend, right?"

I shook my head. "I know." I wasn't ready to reveal all the drama to him, and I hoped Jane hadn't said anything about it to anyone either. It was better to let them think Maggie was Nikos' girlfriend, unless Nikos himself told them otherwise. I didn't want to be the one contradicting Maggie's words.

"Thanks for the advice, Robert. I'll stay away from Nikos, for my own sake. I don't need any problems with Maggie. Besides, he's leaving in a few weeks and this will be over soon," I said. Robert smiled.

"You're a smart girl, and I don't want to see you getting hurt. Greek hunk has every woman in this museum drooling over him and trying to go out with him. Believe me; he doesn't accept anyone's invitation, only Maggie's. And… yours, apparently," he said.

"I haven't invited him anywhere, Robert. All the interaction we've had so far has been due to my project. It's purely professional." I was getting irritated and didn't want to get into details about my relationship with Nikos.

"I'm sorry, sweetie. Don't break your heart over him," Robert said. Jane was unusually quiet and I almost felt her silence meant guilty, but I would deal with her later, not there in front of Robert.

"Well, I'll see you all later. I really need to get going." I got up and walked towards my area, getting rid of my Frappuccino cup in the trash bin by the hallway and feeling relieved to be out of my friends' investigative mood.

By lunch time, Jane came looking for me. "Hey, girlfriend, want to have some lunch or are you having a date with Greek stud?"

"Jane, I'm not really in the mood for the sarcasm. And Robert this morning, what was that all about?" I snapped.

"Sorry. We're just concerned about you..."

"WE? Did you tell everything to Curt and Robert? I can't believe it."

"Well, not exactly. They were probing me with questions. You know how bad at lying I am, but I swear I didn't say much. I just told them you were... how can I say... head over heels for Nikos?"

"Right. As if they needed confirmation. Apparently I can't disguise my feelings for Nikos."

"Don't be mad at us, Sabrina. We're really concerned because of Maggie. Curt and Robert have seen first hand her erratic, crazy, obnoxious, super jealous behavior. I don't know how else to put it but if this woman finds out you're sleeping with her fantasy deity, I can't even imagine what she will do to you."

I sighed. In a way, she was right. Maggie was a threat - a real threat. She wasn't leaving but Nikos was. And I'd have to deal with her, without him to soothe me. "Thanks. I'll keep a distance from him at least while we're here in the museum. We had this conversation before, I know, but believe me, Jane... I can't stay away from Nikos. It's magnetic. I'm powerless in his presence."

"Yeah, I get it. I'll be here for you in a few weeks when you can't stop crying over him, so go ahead and enjoy him while you can. What else can I say?" I hugged her. I couldn't get upset at Jane; after all, she was my best friend who was just trying to look out for me. And I would need a crying shoulder in a few weeks, for sure.

At 2 am, I woke up startled. I couldn't remember if I was having a dream, but once I realized what time it was, I thought of Nikos. He was certainly awake, worried about the museum's jewels transfer. I wanted to call him, talk to him, and make sure he was OK and not so stressed about it. But I wouldn't accomplish much. I might even cause him more upset, especially if he was on the phone talking to his people in Greece. I tried to go back to bed, but insomnia took over. I couldn't get my mind to relax. Hopefully there was nothing to Nikos' feelings concerning the jewels, and we would spend the next night together without worries. I tossed and turned, fantasizing about my Olympian god. I couldn't sleep any longer, so I got dressed and drove to Starbucks on West Gray to grab some coffee and chitchat with Rodney before making my way to the museum.

Even with my stop at Starbucks, I was still early getting to work. I parked the car and stayed inside, finishing my coffee and listening to music, trying to relax, thinking about the day ahead, and looking forward to the night when Nikos would come over and my desire would be satisfied again. I was so lost in my thoughts I almost didn't notice the Jeep Cherokee parking across from me. My Greek hero had just arrived. I put the coffee cup away and was ready to get out of the car to walk in and surprise him, when his passenger door opened and Maggie stepped out. She looked absolutely stunning with a teal sun dress wrapped with a cream colored silk shawl, and wearing strap sandals - definitely not appropriate attire to be volunteering at the museum. It was 7:40 am. My heart pounded erratically inside my chest and my mouth dried up. Nikos came out of the car, wearing black pants and a light blue button down shirt, the sleeves rolled up a bit, the sunglasses making him look like a model from a fashion magazine. He closed the car door and they both crossed the street hurriedly, walking straight into the museum. What was going on? I didn't know what to think. Again, my emotions were in turmoil. Did he spend the night with Maggie? What if this whole thing about the jewels was a lie? Why couldn't I trust him?

I remained inside the car for another ten minutes before composing myself enough to enter the museum and concentrate on my day without ruining it even further. I had started the day with hopes of a wonderful night ahead, and now the dark cloud of doubt and insecurity was overshadowing it. Seeing Maggie and Nikos arriving together in his car, all dressed up, had totally thrown me off balance.

The museum was quiet and almost deserted as it was not open to the public yet for at least another two hours. I dragged myself to my department and started working at once, trying to avoid an imminent depressive mood. Was I over-reacting? I had to be sensible. Why would Nikos lie to me? If Maggie was overseeing her father's projects concerning Nikos' museum, she was going to be around him and I knew that. And last night was an important night, when the Gold Mycenaean Jewelry pieces would be transported to Mr. Wallendorf's friend's private collection. Why couldn't I believe him? I was too jealous of Maggie to be anything but reasonable. Nikos would surely contact me soon to let me know what was happening and to confirm he was coming over tonight. I had to trust him. I wanted to trust him.

"Baby girl, let's go to lunch," I heard Curt calling out to me. I checked my phone, it was already noon. I hadn't even noticed how time had gone by so fast.

"Hi, Curt… I'm not hungry, I'll pass. I'll just work through my lunch today," I said.

"No, baby, you need to come. I have something to tell you that I'm sure you're not aware of yet, and I prefer to be the first one you hear it from," Curt said in a serious tone. It was rare to see Curt seemingly so serious and concerned, and he got me worried.

"What happened? You're scaring me!"

"Let's get out of here. Come with me - Jane and Robert are waiting for us at the Café." I dropped the metal tags I was separating to place on the new displays, picked up my purse from the curator's office and walked with Curt towards the restaurant, taken much by surprise by his urgency in making sure I joined them for lunch. I still wasn't hungry, so I grabbed a glass of water. Robert and Jane were waiting for us in one of the outside tables. It felt weird - they all had a somber look about them, almost as if they were ready to go to a funeral.

"OK, guys, what's going on?" I asked, unable to disguise my curiosity. "Who died?" I tried to lighten up the mood.

"Nikos and Maggie just left for Greece," Curt said bluntly, without blinking. I gaped at him. He must be joking. I had seen them coming in to the museum a few hours ago.

"What... do you m-mean... left... for Greece?" I stuttered.

"I'm sorry, my love. I had to shoot this awful news to you, but I didn't see a better way of doing it," Curt said. Jane reached out for my hand and squeezed it hard.

"You're going to be fine, Sabrina dear, we're all here for you," she said.

"What... do you m-mean... left... for Greece?" I repeated myself, as if I was in a trance, in automatic mode.

"Something bad happened overnight in Greece," Curt said. "Apparently there were some very important artifacts a private collector was going to borrow, and during the transfer, there was a heist. Mr. Wallendorf's a friend of the private collector, and he sent Maggie and Nikos immediately back to Greece in his private plane for them to help out with the investigations. The driver picked them up about 9 am."

The blood drained from my face and I felt lightheaded. I stared at them, unable to say anything. I couldn't believe what Curt was saying. Nikos was on his way to Greece with Maggie, the jewels had been stolen, and I might never ever see him again.

"Sweetheart, I hate to be the one to tell you this, but you would eventually find out," Curt apologized, while he stroked my hair lightly. I choked. Tears filled my eyes and I wanted to disappear. I was speechless - this was too much to bear. My heart ached and I thought it was going to explode inside of me.

"Thank you. Thank you for letting me know before I heard rumors. This is… really unexpected." I didn't know how to react. I was numb but I had to stay strong at least for now and try to hold it inside.

"You're going to be OK, aren't you?" Jane asked me. I could tell she was surprised with my reaction. After all, I wasn't bawling uncontrollably. But I knew what would come later.

"We all knew he would be leaving sooner or later…" I mumbled, still in shock and disbelief. My Olympian dream was gone with Maggie back to Greece, without saying goodbye. Without a word. Without warning. "Does Dr. Jones know? Does he need any help from us filling in for Nikos?" I couldn't believe I had the strength to ask that.

"Dr. Jones is aware and totally upset. There were still a few more weeks of Nikos here, and now he has to cancel a lot of lectures and meetings. He asked me to take Nikos' rental car back. It's somewhere in the parking lot."

"I… I can do that for you after I get off work. I know where he parked."

"Are you sure? That would be great. Here are the keys. I think all his keys are here. Dr. Jones gave me the whole thing in case I had to go to his apartment and return the gate opener."

Curt gave me Nikos' key chain and I stuffed it inside my jeans' pocket. I left them and returned to the gallery. There was no point in going home and dwelling on the inevitable truth. It ached more than I thought such pain could possibly hurt. The unbearable agony of uncertainty, of not knowing if I'd ever see Nikos again in my life was devastating. After working like a robot for the rest of the afternoon, I was glad to leave for the day.

I found the Jeep Cherokee where Nikos had parked it in the morning, across from my car, which he hadn't even noticed. I opened the door, got into the driver's seat, and looked around but the car was spotless, ready to be delivered. There were no signs the car had been used by him. I sat there for a moment, inhaling the intoxicating scent of his powerful and sexy smell still lingering around.

Before driving to the car rental office, I stopped at his apartment complex. The gate opened automatically, since the remote gate opener was still inserted in the sun visor pocket. I parked the car and walked slowly up to his apartment. I was hoping to find him there, waiting for me, telling me all of this had been nothing but a joke. But when I opened the door, Nikos was not there to greet me. I moved slowly around the place, looking for signs of his presence. There was nothing that belonged to him. The apartment was as spotless and as neutral as it was on the night I spent with him not long ago. I didn't know what I was expecting to find, but Nikos was really gone and now this awful reality was getting more and more vivid. I ran from the apartment with tears in my eyes. I had no idea why I was doing that to myself. I should have let Curt take care of this. It was too much to swallow. I got back into the car, stopped in front of the office and went in, carrying the remote gate opener.

"Can I help you?" The woman sitting at the front desk asked upon seeing me enter.

"This is the gate opener for the apartment Nikos Soulis vacated this morning," I said, my voice faltering. I handed her the device. She took it from me and asked me to repeat his name, then looked it up on her computer and typed something.

"Thank you, it's all taken care of. Dr. Soulis was a wonderful tenant. Too bad he had to leave so unexpectedly. Do you have his key?" she asked.

I took his key chain out of my pocket, removed the apartment key and turned it in. "Thank you, have a nice evening. Please tell him we will miss him," the woman said politely. I nodded and left.

I dropped his car at the rental agency and got a ride back to my own car still parked in the museum. I drove home with tears streaming down my face. I had no idea what kind of night was awaiting me. Should I drink myself to sleep? I got inside my apartment and walked towards my bedroom, staring at the empty bed like a pathetic puppet whose strings were cut, paralyzed, frozen, broken. Nikos was not coming tonight. Nikos was not coming any time soon. Nikos might never come back. I heard the buzz of my phone. It was Jane.

"I'm checking on you," she said.

"I don't know what to say. I'm moving, somehow, but it hurts, everything hurts. I'm in a state of denial. I don't know, I'm numb. I never thought it could hurt so much."

"Do you want me to come over and make you company?"

"No, thanks, Jane. I want to be by myself. I'll be fine. I'll try to sleep. But thanks for checking on me, I really appreciate it. Love you, girl."

"Look, if you need me, don't hesitate to call me, any time. I hope you feel better and catch some sleep. I'll see you tomorrow. You were very brave this afternoon."

When I hung up, I realized there was a missed text on the phone. I clicked on it to see what it said. It was an empty text, with a link attached to it. My heart sank. I clicked on the link, and heard the most beautiful and sad song, which Nikos had sent to me. I sobbed in an uncontrollable pain. My heart ached so much I could barely hear Chris Martin's voice over the speaker, painfully singing Coldplay's The Scientist.

All I heard was Nikos' voice telling me it was not easy, telling me how hard it was for us to part. I scrolled down the phone till I found the only picture I had of us together, on a beautiful day in San Antonio that seemed like a million light years ago, when we were so carefree, so happy and so in love. I collapsed in bed, clutching onto my phone, trying to hold on to the memories I had of my Olympian passion.

149

Olympian Passion is the first book in the Olympian trilogy written by romance writer Andrya Bailey. She also writes poetry and fiction as Andrea Barbosa. Follow her on twitter for news of upcoming releases - @AndyB0810.

Coming soon:

Olympian Heartbreak
Olympian Love

Waves of Passion
(anthology featuring No Inhibition, an erotic short story)

Thank you for reading this book. If you enjoyed it, please leave a review on the site where you purchased it from. It's much appreciated. With lots of Olympian passion,
Andrya.

CPSIA information can be obtained
at www.ICGtesting.com
Printed in the USA
LVOW11s1742050418

572435LV00004B/875/P